AT EIGHTEEN CHIP HARRISON HAS ONLY ONE THING ON HIS MIND. . . .

He pursues it first with a young prostitute in Manhattan.

Then he meets a hot, young Georgia girl on a bus ride south.

Next he's playing chess with a madam, footsie with a waitress, and house with an underage cheerleader who's the local fire-and-brimstone preacher's kid.

What Chip has on his mind is writing his second book. Doing the first one nearly got him killed. Now he's looking for new material. But with his predilection for being where he shouldn't and doing just about anything, it's déjà vu all over again—and this aspiring author may end up penning R.I.P.

CHIP HARRISON SCORES AGAIN

CHIP HARRISON
SCORES AGAIN

A CHIP HARRISON NOVEL

Lawrence Block

A SIGNET BOOK

SIGNET
Published by the Penguin Group
Penguin Books USA Inc., 375 Hudson Street,
New York, New York 10014, U.S.A.
Penguin Books Ltd, 27 Wrights Lane,
London W8 5TZ, England
Penguin Books Australia Ltd, Ringwood,
Victoria, Australia
Penguin Books Canada Ltd, 10 Alcorn Avenue,
Toronto, Ontario, Canada M4V 3B2
Penguin Books (N.Z.) Ltd, 182–190 Wairau Road,
Auckland 10, New Zealand

Penguin Books Ltd, Registered Offices:
Harmondsworth, Middlesex, England

Published by Signet, an imprint of Dutton Signet,
a division of Penguin Books USA Inc.

First Signet Printing, April, 1997
10 9 8 7 6 5 4 3 2 1

REGISTERED TRADEMARK—MARCA REGISTRADA

Printed in the United States of America

PUBLISHER'S NOTE
This is a work of fiction. Names, characters, places, and incidents either
are the product of the author's imagination or are used fictitiously, and
any resemblance to actual persons, living or dead, events, or locales is
entirely coincidental.

ONE

AT FIRST I DIDN'T PAY VERY MUCH AT-tention to the guy. I was washing my hands in the men's room of a movie theater on Forty-second Street, and in a place like that it's not an especially good idea to pay too much attention to anybody or you could wind up getting more involved than you might want to. It's not that everybody is a faggot. But everybody figures everybody *else* is a fag-got, so if you let your eyes roam around you could get (*a*) groped by someone who's inter-ested or (*b*) punched in the mouth by some-one who's not interested or (*c*) arrested by someone who's a cop.

If any of these things happened I would

have had to leave the theatre, probably, and I didn't want to. I had already seen both movies, one of them twice, but I still didn't want to leave. It was warm in the theater. Outside it was cold, with day-old snow turning from gray to black, and once I went out there I would have to stay out there, because I had no other place to go.

(Which is not entirely true. There was this apartment on East Fifth Street between Avenues B and C where I could stay if I really had to. Some friends of mine lived there, and while it wasn't exactly a crash pad they would always let me have a section of floor to sleep on and a plate of brown rice to eat. They were into this macrobiotic thing and all they ever ate was brown rice, which is very nourishing and very healthy and very boring after not very long. I could go there and eat and sleep and even talk to people, although most of the people you found there were usually too stoned to say very much, but the thing was that I only had a quarter, which is a nickel less than the subway costs. It was too cold to walk that far, and it was just about as cold inside that place as it was outside, because there was no heat. My friends had been using the stove to heat the place. That hadn't worked too well in the first place, and it worked less well when Con Ed turned off the gas and electricity for nonpayment. They burned candles for light and cooked the rice over little cans of sterno. A couple of times Robbo had burned old furniture in the bathtub for heat, but he had more or less given this up, partly because heating the bathroom didn't do much for the rest of the apartment, and partly because there was a good chance the whole building would go up sooner or later.)

The point of this is just that I was washing my hands and not paying much attention to anything else until I happened to notice this guy take a wallet out of his pocket and start going through it. He was sort of hunched toward me, screening the wallet with his body from the washroom attendant, who I think existed to make sure that if anybody did anything dirty, they did it in one of the pay toilets. The guy with the wallet went through all the compartments of the thing, taking out money and plastic cards and things, and jamming everything into his pockets. Then he put the wallet in another pocket, took out a comb, combed his long dark hair back into a d.a., and left.

I turned and watched him, and on the way out his hand dipped into a pocket and came up with the wallet and dropped it into the wastebasket. There was this huge wastebasket on the opposite side of the door from the washroom attendant, and the guy with the d.a. did this whole number in one graceful motion, and the attendant never saw what happened.

I have to admit that it took me a minute to figure this out. Why would a guy throw his wallet away? And why be so slick about it? I mean, if you grow tired of your wallet, you have a perfect right to throw it away, right?

Oh.

It wasn't his wallet. He was a pickpocket or a mugger or something, and he had emptied the wallet, and now he wanted to get rid of it because it was Incriminating Evidence.

How about that.

My first reaction was just general excitement. Not that I had been an eyewitness to the most spectacular crime since the Brink's robbery. I would guess they get more wallets in those wastebaskets than they get paper towels. In fact, if you ever want a used wallet, that's probably the best place to go looking for one. But my own life hadn't been that thrilling lately, and it didn't take much to make my day.

The next thing that struck me was that I, Chip Harrison, had just been presented with an opportunity. A small one, perhaps, but I was as low on opportunities as I was on excitement. And that wallet was an opportunity.

It might hold important papers, for example. You might argue that people with important papers in their wallets don't spend all that much time in Forty-second Street movie houses, but one never knows for sure. Perhaps the owner would pay a reward for the return of the wallet. (Perhaps he'd call the police and have me arrested as a pickpocket.) Or perhaps there was some small change in the change compartment, if there was a change compartment. Or a subway token. Or a postage stamp. The Post Office won't redeem unused stamps, but at least I could mail a letter, if there was someone I wanted to write to. Or perhaps—

Well, there were endless possibilities.

I mulled them over in my mind while I was

drying my hands on a paper towel, and I looked at the attendant and at the wastebasket, and then I went out and combed my hair again. I had just done this before washing my hands in the first place and while my hair tends to need combing frequently it didn't really need it now. But I was about to Take Advantage of Opportunity, and thus I had to Think On My Feet.

I dried my hands again, and I carried the used paper towel over to the wastebasket, keeping the comb in the same hand with it, and I dropped them both into the basket.

Then I took a step or two toward the door, stopped abruptly, made a fist of one hand and hit the palm of the other hand with it.

"Oh, shit," I said. "I dropped my comb in the wastebasket."

"I seen you," the attendant said.

"All the stupid things."

"You want another comb, there's a machine over on the side."

"I want *that* comb," I said.

"Prob'ly dirty by now. You wouldn't believe the crap they throw in those baskets."

"I think I can get it." I was leaning into the basket and pawing around through old

Kleenex and paper towels. The wallet had plummeted through them to the bottom, and I was having a hell of a time finding it.

"Over there," the clown said helpfully. "You see it?"

I did, damn him. I pawed at some paper towels and made the comb slip away. "Almost had it," I said, and went diving for it again. I had my feet off the ground and was balanced rather precariously, with the edge of the can pushing my belt buckle through my stomach. I had visions of losing my balance and winding up headfirst in the trashcan, which might provide some people with some laughs but which wouldn't provide me with the wallet, the comb, or much in the way of self-respect.

And self-respect, at that point of time, was as hard to come by as excitement, opportunity, and money.

I kept my balance and after another few shots I got the wallet. I can't swear that it's the same wallet I saw go in. For all I know there were a dozen of them somewhere down there. I got *a* wallet, palmed it off, and slipped it inside my shirt, and then I had to go through the charade of getting the fucking comb. It just didn't seem right to leave it there.

On my way through the lobby I dumped the comb in yet another wastebasket. And did it very surreptitiously, as if I were, well, a pickpocket ditching a wallet. Which is nothing but stupid.

I went outside and walked down to Broadway and watched the news flashing on the Allied Chemical Tower. It was cold, and there was a miserable wind blowing off the Hudson. I stood there shivering. I was out in the cold with no way of getting back into the warm, and I had traded a perfectly adequate pocket comb for a wallet that someone else had already gone through once, and I wasn't entirely certain I had come out ahead on the deal.

The papers in that wallet weren't important enough to wrap fish in. There were a couple of cash register receipts from unidentified stores and a Chinese laundry ticket. There was a head-and-shoulders snapshot of an ugly high school girl signed *Your Pal, Mary Beth Hawkins*. Judging by the hair style, Mary Beth was either (*a*) the squarest teen-ager in

America or (b) forty-five-years old by now. Either way, I would have rather had my comb than her picture.

There were a few other things, but none of them mattered except for the bus ticket. It was in one of the secret compartments, and I guess that had kept it a secret from the pickpocket. A Greyhound bus ticket, good for one-way passage in either direction between Boston, Massachusetts, and Bordentown, South Carolina. It said it was valid anytime within one year from the date stamped on the back. The date was March something, and it was now December something, so the ticket had another three months to go before it became even more worthless than it already was.

I got rid of the rest of the wallet, Mary Beth's picture and all. I dumped it in a trash-can—what else?—and I was as slick as possible about this, because I didn't want any other poor clown to waste his time doing what I had just done. If you're going to steal a wallet, you ought to get it from its original owner. After that the depreciation is fantastic.

Then I walked around for a while, which kept me warmer than standing still, if just barely. Now and then I would take the ticket out and stare at it. It was that or stare at the quarter. Sensational, I thought. If I happen to be in Boston between now and March, I can catch a bus to Bordentown. Or, should I some fine morning find myself in Bordentown, I can hop on a Greyhound for Boston. Wonderful.

I wound up on Broadway looking at whores. Not in a particularly acquisitive way. Not that I wasn't tempted. I had been in New York for almost three months, and my sex life during that time could have been inscribed on the head of a pin with plenty of room left for the Lord's Prayer and as many angels as felt like dancing there.

(I had been living with a girl for one of those months, but she had just had a baby and couldn't do anything for six weeks, and by the time the six weeks were up she had gone away. At least she took the baby with her.)

I have always had these ethical objections to patronizing a prostitute, but in this case I might have overcome these objections if I'd had more than twenty-five cents to overcome them with. We'll never know.

So I went window-shopping, and the girls

seemed to know it. They would look me up and down, and disapproval would glint in their eyes, and they would turn away, as if there was nothing so obvious as the fact that I couldn't possibly afford them. None of this was very ego-building.

And then one girl, who was either less experienced or a poorer judge of character, gave me a smile. An actual smile. So I stopped dead and smiled back at her, and she asked me if I'd like to go to her apartment.

"Is it warm there?"

"Honey," she said, "where I am, it's always warm."

I told her it sounded great. She asked me if I could spend twenty-five dollars.

"No way."

"Well, see, I like you. Could you spend twenty?"

"I wish I could."

"Well, shit. What *can* you spend?"

I could spend twenty-five cents, but I was damned if I was going to tell her that. I said, "Where are you from?"

"What do you want to know that for?"

"I just wondered."

15

"Well, I have this place on Fifty-fifth Street. How much can—"

"I mean originally," I said. "You're not from New York, are you?"

"From Memphis," she said. "And never goin' back there again, thanks all the same."

"Oh," I said.

"Why?"

"I thought maybe you were from Bordentown, South Carolina," I said. "Or maybe from Boston."

"You been drinkin', honey?"

"Because I have this bus ticket," I said, and showed it to her. "So if you had any interest in going to Boston or Bordentown—"

"That good?"

I showed her the date. "Perfectly good," I said.

"You want to come home with me?"

"To Memphis?"

"Shit. I tol' you. Fifty-fifth Street. You want to come?"

I tried on a smile. "All I really have is this ticket," I said. "I don't have any money. Just twenty-five cents and this ticket. I'm sorry for wasting your time—"

But she had my arm tucked under hers.

16

"You know something? I like you. I really do. What's your name?"

"Chip."

"Yeah? I'm Mary Beth. What's the matter?"

"Nothing. I knew a girl named Mary Beth. I had a picture of her in a wallet that I carried for a while."

"Girl here in New York?"

"No," I said. "I think she lives in Bordentown. Or in Boston. Or she used to."

"You sure you all right?"

"I'm fine," I said. She was still holding onto my arm, and we seemed to be walking uptown, sort of toward Fifty-fifth Street, actually.

"I do like you, Chip," she was saying. "You just come home with me and I'll do you like you never been done. You ever had something called the Waterloo? That's a specialty of mine. What I take is a mouthful of warm water, see—"

She told me quite a bit about the Waterloo, and while she talked we walked, and while we walked she held onto my arm and rubbed it against her breast. My pants began getting very cramped.

"You just forget about no money," she said. "Don't make no never mind."

17

LAWRENCE BLOCK

Oh, Jesus, I thought. I can't believe this.

Because I couldn't. I mean, it wasn't as though I hadn't had thoughts along this line before. I don't suppose it's the rarest fantasy ever. The ultimate sexual ego trip—that a prostitute, a girl who spends her life getting paid to have sex, will find you so overwhelmingly attractive that she'll want to give it to you for free. And she would know tricks you never dreamed of, and do all these fantastic things, and do them all for love.

Who ever thought it would actually happen?

Her apartment was pleasant in a sort of dull way. I couldn't tell whether or not it was a typical prostitute's apartment, but it seemed to me then that it couldn't be, because it seemed to me then that she was by no means a typical prostitute. By the time we got there I had already decided that she wasn't basically a whore at all. Just because a girl was whoring didn't make her a whore. After all, in the past year I had sold termite extermination service, picked fruit, posed for pornographic pictures and written a book, and I didn't think of myself as a writer or fruitpicker or any of those things. Life deals unpredictable

18

cards, and you have to play each hand as it lays, and little Mary Beth might be walking the streets but that didn't make her a street-walker. It might not make her the Virgin Mary, either, but it didn't make her a whore.

I really had things all figured out. I would Take Her Away From All This. She already loved me, and by the time I got done balling her she would love me to distraction, and at that point the idea of ever having sex with anyone but Chip Harrison would positively turn her stomach. And I would live with her and land a Job With A Future, and we would screw incessantly while I made my way in the world, and we would, uh, Live Happily Ever After.

The things is, see, that when a fantasy starts coming true before your eyes, it's natural to go on taking the fantasy to its logical (?) conclusion. Did I really expect all of this would happen? Not really, but remember that I never expected it to start happening in the first place. If someone goes and repeals the Law of Gravity and you find yourself flying to the Moon, it's no more unreasonable to plan on flying clear through to Mars.

I stood there working all of this out while

she closed the door and turned four or five locks. Doesn't want us to be interrupted, I thought happily. We might be here for days. Weeks. And she wants to make sure we have privacy.

"Well," she said. "Not much, but it's home."

"Mary Beth," I said.

"Hi, Chip."

"Mary Beth." And I put my hands on her shoulders and drew her close. Somewhere along the way her head turned to the side and I was kissing a gold hoop earring.

"Uh-uh," she said.

"Huh?"

She rubbed her breasts against my chest and bounced her groin playfully against mine. I had this tight feeling in my chest.

"I don't kiss on the mouth," she said.

"Huh?"

She gave me another happy bounce, then moved away. "Just something I don't do," she said. "Kiss you anywheres else, kiss you like nobody ever, but not on the mouth."

"But that's silly."

"Shit—"

"But—"

I remembered reading that some prostitutes refused to kiss their clients mouth-to-mouth. They would do anything else, but they reserved that intimacy for the men they loved. It had never made much sense to me at the time, because if you stop and think about it, well, it's pretty ridiculous. Especially since I had spent the past year with a lot of girls who would kiss you mouth-to-mouth until Rome fell but wouldn't do anything more exciting than that. It seemed as though the whores had their value system turned upside down.

But what I couldn't understand was what this had to do with me and Mary Beth. She didn't want money from me. She was doing this for love, so by rights she should be particularly keen on kissing me on the mouth.

And then I got it. The poor kid, I realized, had never really had any sex life to speak of outside of prostitution. So naturally that was her frame of reference. Here she wanted to ball me for the sheer unadulterated pleasure of it, but her mind was so conditioned by the life she led that she had to act with me in much the same way as she acted with her paying customers. It was weird, and sort of disheartening in a way, but there was also something sort of sweet and pathetic about it.

She has never known love, I told myself. But I shall change her. I shall fulfill her.

"Well, now," she said. "And what have we here?"

That must have been a rhetorical question, because what she had there was something she came into contact with quite frequently in her profession, and where we had it was in her hand. She had opened my fly and taken me firmly in hand, and she was stroking me rhythmically. Her wrist did everything; the rest of her arm stayed motionless.

"You come with me," she said. "We'll just wash you up first."

We stood at the bathroom sink and washed me up. The editorial *we* was bugging me a little. Nurses talk like that—"How are we feeling this morning?"—but I never figured whores did, too. Anyway, she soaped me up and rinsed me off, and it was sort of pleasant and unpleasant both at once, pleasant in that it felt good, and unpleasant in that it sort of implied that I was fundamentally too dirty to deal with otherwise. But then I thought of some of the things she had in mind, and some of the things she had done with other people, and I decided I was just as glad that she tended to wash this portion of a person beforehand, and also, to tell the truth, just as pleased that she didn't believe in mouth-to-mouth kissing.

When she was done she filled a glass with hot water and carried it into the bedroom. "For the Waterloo," she explained. "You're gonna love this."

"Uh."

"Don't you want to take off your clothes, Chip?"

"Uh, sure," I said, and started undressing. I was feeling unbelievably dizzy and stupid, and it wasn't just the excitement. That was a part of it. But another part was the feeling that none of this was really happening. It all seemed so thoroughly unreal. I took off all my clothes and looked up and she was just standing there, with her clothes on.

"Your clothes," I said.

"Huh?"

"Why don't you, uh, get undressed?"

"You want me to?"

"Well, sure."

She shrugged. A very strange girl, I decided. Maybe it wasn't just that she hadn't had any real sex life outside of prostitution. Maybe she was equally inexperienced *in* prostitution. Maybe she just read about the Waterloo in a book or something.

I stood there watching while she got undressed. She didn't make the process particularly seductive, just shucked off her clothes and draped them over a chair. Her body was skimpy everywhere but the breasts, which were on the large size. I haven't described her too much because I have trouble picturing her now in my mind. She was sort of mousy, really, hair somewhere between blond and brown. I suppose she was around my age, although she seemed older, maybe because she was more at home in this scene than I was.

She left on her stockings and garter belt. I asked her if she didn't want to take them off and get comfortable, and she gave me an impatient look. "Most men like 'em on," she said. "Don't you think they look pretty?"

I thought they looked like something out of those whip-and-chain movies, but I said sure, they were pretty.

"Because it's wasting time, you know, taking 'em off, putting 'em on."

"Then leave them on," I said, and she nodded, and I reached out for her and drew her in close. I went to kiss her again, out of habit, but she turned away automatically and I didn't press the point. I sort of felt like apologizing but couldn't think of an intelligent way to do that, so I kept my mouth shut and let my fingers do the walking. I felt various parts of her, and she did a little deep breathing and such, but nothing that really assured me I was driving her out of her skull.

"Let me," she said, disengaging herself. "You just lay down, Chip, and let me do you up."

I got on the bed. She reached for the glass of water, then stopped with it halfway to her lips. "You tell me if it's too hot," she said.

Then she took a mouthful of water and bent over me.

It was really very nice. She just did it for a second or so, then pulled away and looked at me. I was waiting for her to ask me whatever the hell it was she was going to ask me, and then I realized that she wasn't going to ask me anything because she couldn't because she had her mouth full of hot water.

"It's not too hot," I said. "It's just right."

She nodded and started doing it again.
And, as before, it was really very nice indeed.
It was strange, too, because I felt totally un-
connected with the whole process. I decided
that it was a great technique, and it was really
great that she knew these great techniques,
but that it would be infinitely better when I
taught her how to put some love into the
whole process. Or at least to make it obvious
to me that she was enjoying what she was
doing.

Then she stopped again.

"Believe me, it's not too hot," I said, and
started to push her head back in place. But
her head wouldn't push. She leaned over and
spat the water out onto the linoleum.

"The ticket," she said.

"Huh?"

She looked impatient again. "The bus
ticket, man. You better give it to me now. I
want to make sure it's still good."

"The bus ticket?"

She sat up and stared at me. "Shit, the *bus*
ticket," she said. "What's the matter with
you? You got to give it to me and I got to
make sure I can cash it before we do any
more. All I need is—"

"Cash the bus ticket?"

"Take it over to Port Authority and cash it," she said. "I told you you didn't need money. Just the ticket is all. If it's good I'll get twenty-thirty dollars out of that ticket."

I suppose you saw it coming all along, but I'm not going to apologize for my stupidity. After all, it was *my* fantasy that we were acting out.

The Waterloo, I thought. I had already had the hot water part, and now I was getting the cold water. Buckets of it, all over all my enthusiasm for little old Mary Beth.

"Hey! Where you goin'?"

I was putting on my clothes. Not too quickly, not too slowly. Very mechanically, actually. Tucking the shirt into the pants, getting my socks right-side out and then putting them on, then the shoes—

"You crazy?"

"I have to go," I said.

"Go? Where to?"

"The bus station," I said. "I have to cash the ticket."

"Shit, I said I would cash it. Just hand it on over here."

"Fuck you," I said.

27

"Are you out of your *mind*?"

I turned toward her, and I guess I must have wanted to kill her, or at least I looked as though I wanted to kill her, because her face drained of color and she backed off fast. I turned away from her again and went to the door.

The whore with the heart of gold. You didn't need money. All you needed was a negotiable bus ticket.

I almost went crazy unlocking all those locks. She never said a word, which was lucky for her. I'm normally about as nonviolent as it's possible to get, but I wasn't feeling very normal just then. Nothing makes you hate a person quite so much as being made an absolute asshole out of.

The last lock cleared just as I was about to give up and kick the door down.

It was as cold as ever out there, but I walked three blocks before I even noticed it.

Two thoughts kept me from running around and screaming. One was that, if and when I calmed down, I was certain to see the humor in the situation. I didn't see any humor in it now, but I knew I would sooner or later.

The other comforting thought, and it was the more comforting of the two, was that I had that bus ticket in my pocket. And I could cash it in.

TWO

THIS IS SORT OF A PROBLEM.

See, I was going to open the book by saying who I am and my background and all the rest of it and get that out of the way right at the start. But the thing is that I wrote one book before this. It was called *No Score*, and it just came out last month. Gold Medal published it. *No Score*, by Chip Harrison. That wasn't what I wanted to call it, but forget what I wanted to call it because they changed it. I think *No Score* is a pretty good title, catchy, and probably a lot better than what I had in mind.

The point is that some of you already read *No Score* and some of you didn't, and if you did read it maybe you still remember it and maybe you don't. I remember it very clearly, but that's different.

See, if you read *No Score*, I don't want to bore you by feeding you all that stuff here and there throughout this book. If you didn't read it, I want to tell you as much as you have to know about it, but at the same time I don't want to spoil it for you in case you by some chance enjoy this book and want to read *No Score* later on. Of course the best thing would be if you ran out right now and got a copy of *No Score* and read it first and then came back to this book, but obviously not everybody can do that. If they happen to be reading this on a plane, for instance.

So what I think I'll do is put down some of it right here and now to tell you as much as you have to know about me, and possibly more than you want to know, as far as that goes. If you did read *No Score*, you can skip ahead right now to the next chapter, because none of this will be news to you.

*   *   *

My name is Chip Harrison. I guess you know that. My legal name was originally Leigh Harvey Harrison, but Chip was my nickname from early childhood, and my parents decided in November of 1963 that it might be sensible to forget my legal name and concentrate on Chip, Leigh Harvey being a liability in the name market at that point in time.

Of course, that was so many assassinations ago I don't suppose it matters any more.

No Score opened when I was seventeen and in my last semester at Upper Valley Prep School. I found out then that my parents had been confidence swindlers, and they were about to go to prison, and they committed suicide. I wasn't allowed to finish school, partly because of the scandal and partly because there was no money to pay my bills and I wasn't a good enough basketball player to make a difference, although I was fairly tall for my age.

So I went out to seek my fortune. I went to Chicago and got a job passing out slingers for a sidewalk photographer, and not quite sleeping with his wife, and then I went down through Illinois and Indiana with a termite inspection crew, and almost went to jail for statutory rape, which would have been really weird because (*a*) I was underage myself and (*b*) I didn't get to do anything. Then I wound up picking berries and apples across Ohio and New York, and almost got shot by a jealous husband, which also would have been ironic because (*a*) it wasn't his wife and (*b*) I didn't get to do anything.

In a way, not getting to do anything was what *No Score* was all about. That did work itself out, though, with a surprise touchdown in the final minutes of play. And then I happened to meet Mr. Knox Burger, and he bought me a hamburger because I helped him change a tire on his car, and I got to talking about my experiences and he suggested writing a book. He even gave me fifty dollars so that I could buy a typewriter and live on Maine sardines and day-old bread while I wrote the book. That book turned out to be *No Score*, and when it was done I took it to New York, and in September of 1970 it finally came out. I got some money when I finished the book but not as much as I thought and it didn't last long. It lasted until December, actually, at which time I had twenty-five cents left.

(I don't want to get hung up in time sequences, but let me get the chronology of this down for you. I started writing *No Score* in September of 1969 and finished it about a month later. From October to December of 1969 I was living in New York in the East Village, partly with the girl I mentioned who had just had a baby, and partly here and partly there, and partly at the sort of crash pad where they had all the brown rice and burned chairs in the bathtub. That's when the action in this book starts, in December of 1969. Then in September of 1970 *No Score* was finally published—I don't know why those things take so long, really—and it is now October of 1970 and I am sitting here writing *this* book, which you are reading. God knows when it will be when you get to read it. 1984, probably. In fact it may be close to then by the time I finish this chapter, because it's really very difficult trying to get all this together.

(Actually it may not come out at all, because Mr. Burger doesn't even work there any more. He left, probably because of the nervous strain of editing *No Score*. There's a Mr. Walter Fultz there now, and he gave me about the same advice Mr. Burger did. Keep it moving, he said. Keep it warm and sensitive and perceptive and lively, and most of all—make sure there's sex in it.

(I don't know how well it's moving. Not too well in this chapter because of all the boring recapitulation. I really hope most of you already read *No Score* and were able to skip all of this crap. But I promise the pace will pick up in the next chapter. It would almost have to.

(And I also promise that there will be plenty of sex in it. There really can't help being plenty of sex in it. That's why I decided to start this book in December instead of picking up where *No Score* left off. There were those three months when nothing happened, so I decided to skip them and start right when things started to happen.)

So that's who I am. Not the seventeen-year-old virgin who was there for the start of *No Score*, but an eighteen-year-old virgin-once-removed. A Virgo, with Gemini rising and Moon in Leo, if you pay attention to things like that. Sort of tall and sort of thin and sort of ordinary-looking, and walking full speed through the slush to the Port Authority Bus Terminal.

THREE

THE PORT AUTHORITY BUS TERMINAL IS a well-lighted and spacious modern building, and if you walk through it quickly in the daytime it just looks like a bank or an airport. But at night it's depressing. All bus stations are. It's the people. Half of them are only there because they don't have enough money to fly or take a train, and the other half are there because it's reasonably warm and the benches are reasonably comfortable and you can steal a nap there and other people will think maybe you're waiting for a bus, and will leave you alone. Sooner or later, though, some uniformed old fart will ask you for a ticket, and when you don't have one they tell you to go away.

I didn't have any trouble cashing the ticket. I was in line behind a fat woman whose luggage was a matched set of shopping bags. She wanted to go someplace in Missouri, and she and the clerk had a hell of a job working out the details. This gave me time to figure out various reasons why I was cashing the ticket, but when my turn came I just pushed the ticket through the window and asked for cash. The clerk looked at it as if he suspected I was part of a gang of counterfeiters specializing in old bus tickets. But it passed.

You know, if it hadn't, I really would have been irritated. I mean, the ticket would at least have gotten me Mary Beth.

Instead it got me thirty-seven dollars and eighty-three cents. I went to one of the benches and sat down and counted the money over and over again. Then I put different amounts in different pockets. I was somehow more conscious of pickpockets than ever before. It occurred to me that I could have kept the wallet, and if I had then I'd now have something to put the money in.

Thirty-seven dollars and eighty-three cents. I sat there with different portions of the money in different pockets for a long time, thinking of one thing and another. Then I went to the john. The free stall was in use so I had to use one of the pay toilets, but the attendant wasn't there so I crawled under it. (Under the door. Not under the toilet.)

There should be a law against pay toilets.

I did some more thinking, in addition to doing what I had gone there to do, and I bought a comb for a quarter and combed my hair. The comb lost a couple teeth in the process. It was really shoddy compared to the one I'd thrown away.

Then I went back to the ticket window. "Bordentown, South Carolina," I said. "One way."

The clerk started hunting for the Bordentown tickets, then did an elaborate double take. "You were just here a minute ago," he said.

"Well, maybe fifteen minutes."

"You cashed in a ticket. A Bordentown ticket."

"I know."

"And now you want to buy it back?"

"That was a Boston-to-Bordentown ticket," I said. "What I want is a New York-to-Bordentown ticket."

"Whyntcha just trade it in the first place and save me the aggravation?"

"I didn't realize that I wanted to go to Bordentown."

"What are you, a wise guy?"

"Can't I just buy a ticket?"

"You people. I don't know. Think everybody's got all the time in the world."

The fare from New York to Bordentown was thirty-three dollars and four cents, and I had to go through various pockets until I got that sum together. While I did this, he talked to himself. He wouldn't tell me when the next bus left. I had to use one of the house phones and call Information. They told me there was a bus leaving in two and a half hours. It made express stops from New York to Raleigh, then made local stops all the way to Miami. It would put me in Bordentown in a little over forty hours.

The only thing I knew about Bordentown was that it was in South Carolina, and that somebody named Mary Beth Hawkins probably lived there once. And that I evidently wanted to go there.

I had four dollars and seventy-nine cents left. That was a lot less than thirty-three dollars and four cents, but it was a lot more than a quarter, so I was ahead of the game and playing on the house's money.

I was also starving. I found a lunch counter in the building and had two hamburgers and an order of french fries and three cups of coffee. It certainly wasn't a macrobiotic meal. It wasn't even very good, but that didn't seem to matter. I ate everything but the napkin.

Why Bordentown?

That's a good question. I don't know if I can find an answer that's as good as the question.

See, what happened was that I sat, first on the bench and then on the toilet, and I thought about the money and tried to think of something to do with it. And none of the things that involved staying in New York seemed like very good ideas, and I came to the conclusion that I had bombed out in New York and it was time to go somewhere else. Nothing against the city. Any city or town is as good as or as bad as what you're doing and the people you're doing it with. And for one reason or another I had never quite managed to get it together in New York. There were some good times in among the bad times, and I was glad I had come, but it was time to split.

(I have this tendency to go someplace else whenever I don't like where I am. I never really had a home that I can remember. When I was with my parents we would stay at a different expensive hotel in a different city every couple of months, and when I was at school it was a different boarding school every year, and the pattern hasn't changed since. Sometimes I think it's weakness of character to pick up and run whenever things turn sour. But why stay where you don't want to be? For Pete's sake, there's a whole world out there. I suppose there are things to be said for settling down and sinking roots, but someone else will have to say them.)

The thing is, it's not enough to have someplace to go away from. You also need someplace to go away *to*. And I didn't have one. There were places I had already been, but I couldn't see any point in going back to any of them. Chicago was vaguely possible, I had had reasonably good times there, but I thought about that wind coming off Lake Michigan and schussing through the Loop and imagined what that wind would be like in January, and that ruled out Chicago. Besides, it was too big, it would be too much like what I was leaving.

There was a girl named Hallie with whom I had traded virginities on the very best night of my life. She was in college in Wisconsin. I had sent her a postcard before coming to New York, and since then I had written her three or four stupid letters but never mailed any of them, maybe because I wasn't quite sure what I wanted to say to her. I decided that it would be nice to see Hallie again, and then I decided it would be even nicer to see Hallie when I was a little clearer on how I felt about her and what I wanted to do about it. It would also be nicer if I could see her with clean clothes on me and money in my pocket and a little firmer sense of direction.

And then it came to me.

Bordentown.

Maybe you've noticed that when you've gone without sleep and food for a long time, and without really talking to anybody, you start to get messages from God. That's a little less crazy than it sounds. What happens is that a lot of minor things start taking on tremendous significance, and you start reading vital messages into them.

Like the whole bit with the wallet. And what was in the wallet—a picture of Mary Beth Hawkins and a bus ticket. And the first person I met after that was also named Mary Beth, which may be less remarkable in the cold light of dispassionate analysis but which seemed extraordinary at the time. The way all these things seemed to add up was that it was meant for me to get that bus ticket. It was destiny. And for me to cash in the ticket and spend the money was spitting in destiny's face. Obviously the thing to do with that ticket was to use it and go where it went.

Which still gave me two choices, actually. Boston or Bordentown. But I never seriously considered Boston. It would have been copping out. I mean, the ticket was about eighty-five percent New York-to-Bordentown and fifteen percent New York-to-Boston.

Besides, Boston would be as cold as New York, maybe even colder. And Bordentown was in South Carolina—I knew that much about it, dammit. It would be warm. And it would be a small town, it would have to be fairly small or I probably would have heard

of it at one time or another. So if I was looking for a change from New York, I really
didn't have to look any farther.

For Pete's sake, I've gone lots of places on
less reason than that.

The bus ride started off horrible. Then it
became very boring for a while, and then it
got wonderful.

The horrible part was brief, from New York
to Philadelphia. It was horrible because there
were four men two rows back drinking wine
and singing, and a third of the way to Philadelphia one of them threw up, and a few
miles later so did the rest of them. It was horrible because the woman across the aisle from
me was carrying a baby who cried all the way
from New York to Philadelphia. The woman
didn't seem to mind. Me, I minded. It was
horrible because the man in the seat next to
me was fat enough to take up all of his seat
and a good deal of mine as well. He didn't
use Dial, and I don't guess he cared if anybody else did, either.

The four drunks got off in Trenton. The
woman with the brat got off in Philadelphia.
The smelly fat man was riding clear down to
Miami, but when we got to Philadelphia I was

able to change my seat. So that ended the horrible part.

The boring part was just boring. Nothing much to be said about it, really. I took crumby naps and woke up and went to the john and came back and sat down and looked out the window and waited for something to happen. Now and then the bus stopped somewhere and we all got off it and went to a terrible lunch counter, and I would have a Coke and a package of those little orange crackers with cheese and peanut butter between them.

(I knew a speed freak in New York who lived on nothing but Cokes and those sandwich crackers. Three packs of the crackers a day and six Cokes. He weighed about eighty-three pounds and the circles under his eyes looked as though they'd been painted on with shoe polish. "Speed doesn't kill," he told me. "That's the lie they feed you. It's the malnutrition that does you in. I figure I've got six months before my liver goes. Once your liver goes you've had it."

("Then why don't you start eating right?"

("Priorities, man. I need to speed to get my head together. Once my head is together I'll kick the speed and stabilize myself with tranks and downs, and then I'll get into eating right. High-protein, fertile eggs, the whole organic foods trip. And I want to get into body-building. I've been getting all these catalogues of barbell equipment. But first I have to get my head together. I figure I can get my head together in six months. I figure my liver can make it that long."

(Sure.)

The wonderful part, the part that was not at all horrible or boring, started sometime in the late afternoon and somewhere south of Washington. I don't know the time because I wasn't wearing a watch, and I don't know the name of the town or even the state because I wasn't paying all that much attention to where we were when she joined us. We stopped at some station and I didn't feel like another Coke so I stayed in my seat with my eyes closed. Then just as the bus was starting up a voice said, "Pardon me?" and I looked up and there she was.

She was a little thing, with yellow hair to her shoulders and large round brown eyes and a pointed chin. She was wearing a plaid mini skirt that got halfway to her knee and a cardigan sweater the color of her hair. She had a coat over one arm and was carrying a little suitcase.

At first glance she looked about sixteen. When you looked a little closer at her eyes and the corners of her mouth you could add maybe ten years to that. Say twenty-five.

"Could y'all tell me if this seat is taken?"

It wasn't. Neither were half the seats on the bus, which had emptied out a good deal in Washington. She could have had a whole double seat to herself, actually.

"And could I ask you to help me with this suitcase here?"

It was small and light. I put it in the overhead rack, and then she took a book and a package of cigarettes from her coat pocket and gave me the coat, and I put it alongside the suitcase. I sat down again and she sat down next to me. She didn't have any makeup on except maybe a trace of lipstick, but she was wearing quite a bit of perfume. She smelled very nice, actually. It made me think of Mary Beth, the bus-ticket hooker. Mary Beth had been wearing perfume and hadn't smelled very terrific at all. There's perfume and there's perfume.

"Well, now! I thought we might have rain, but it's turned a nice day after all, hasn't it?"

"Just so there's no snow."

"You from up No'th?"

"I'm not exactly from anywhere," I said. "I was in New York for the past few months."

"And what place do you call home?"

"Wherever I am."

Her face lit up. "Now that's exciting," she said. What she said was *excitin'*, actually, but I hate it when writers spell everything phonetically to get across the fact that somebody has an accent. I'll just say now that she had an accent thicker than spoonbread and you can bear that in mind when you run her dialogue through your head.

"When you don't have one home in particular, why, it's like you're never *away*! Me, I'm an old homebody. My aunt has the pleurisy and I was up doing for her for onto ten days, but except when she has it bad I never get away from home."

"Where's home?"

"Georgia. Mud Kettle, Georgia. Ever been there?"

"No."

"Well, it's not that you missed much." This

I believed. The name wasn't Mud Kettle, by the way, but I looked up the town she mentioned in an atlas just now and the population is less than twenty-five hundred, so I changed the name to Mud Kettle because otherwise somebody could probably figure out who she was, and it might shake up the old folks at home. "Not missing much at all. Well, here I am, little old Willie Em Weeks from Mud Kettle, G-A. Lordy!"

"What does the *M* stand for?" I mean, girls don't usually announce middle initials.

"Emily," she said.

"Emily starts with an *E*," I said.

"Doesn't stand for, it's *short* for! You silly. Willamina Emily Weeks, and isn't that a handle."

Then she waited expectantly, and it occurred to me to tell her my name. She had never met anyone named Chip before, and I had never met any Willie Em, and we got what conversational mileage we could out of that. Which wasn't much.

Then she said, "Chip? Would you mind awfully if I asked you a favor? Would you change seats with me?"

If she wanted to sit by a window, there

were windows all over the place she could pick. I didn't tell her this. I changed seats with her, and our bodies bumped a little in passing. Nothing fantastic, just enough to put ideas in my head.

Which was ridiculous, I thought, sitting down again. She would be fun to talk to, someone to break the monotony of the trip, but that was obviously as far as it was going to go. I was getting off in South Carolina and she was riding clear on to Georgia. And anyway she was married, there was a ring on her finger. And besides that we were on a *bus*, for Pete's sake, in the middle of the afternoon, and all you can do on a bus is sweat and sleep, with sweating considerably more likely than sleeping.

We talked a little more. She asked if I minded if she smoked, and I said I didn't, and she lit a cigarette and opened her book and I settled back in my seat and closed my eyes. I was just as glad she was reading because she wasn't that outstanding to talk to. It was nice watching her and listening to her voice, a very pleasant voice, but it was very hard to concentrate on what she was saying.

So I thought I would doze off again into

that sort of half sleep that's possible on a bus, but I couldn't manage it. It was her, the perfume, the presence. I was aware of her. Somehow I was more aware of her now when she wasn't talking and I wasn't looking at her than I had been before.

After a while she said, "Chip? Are you asleep?"

"No."

"Could you do me a favor?"

She was very large on favors. I opened my eyes. "Sure," I said.

She handed me her book, her finger indicating a place on the page. "Starting right here," she said. "Could you just read that scene?"

"Out loud?"

"No, silly."

I took the book and started to read, and the first thing I did was start blinking furiously. The book was called either *The Swinging Swappers* or *The Swapping Swingers*. It hardly matters which. And the scene she had given me involved six people in a sexual tangle, with everybody doing everything to everybody else, and all in the crudest and most explicit sort of writing. Absolute hard-core pornography. The scene went on for God knows how many pages. I stopped after two and a half of them, and it was just gathering momentum.

And so was I.

I don't know whether I actually blush or not, but if I do, I was doing it then. I closed the book and turned very very slowly to look at her. The expression on her face surprised me. Very serious and matter-of-fact, with a little vertical furrow in the center of her forehead.

"Did you read it?"

"Uh, a couple of pages, yeah."

"You read fast. Could y'all tell me something?"

"What?"

"Was that there an erotic scene? Was it exciting?"

"Yes."

"It was?"

"Uh, yeah. Yes, I would say that you would have to call that an erotic scene. Yes."

Her face relaxed and she gave a little sigh. "Well, that's good news," she said. "See, I thought maybe it was just the bus that was getting to me. I always get so randy on buses. I swear I get like a mare in heat just from riding on a bus. I don't rightly know what it is that does it. The rhythm of the wheels?"

"Maybe."

"You think that could be it?"

"I suppose."

She nodded thoughtfully. "I can feel it right now," she said. "The rhythm of the wheels on my backside."

From her tone of voice we could have been discussing the weather. *Think it'll rain? Oh, most likely not. Course we're due for a little rain. Yes, and I always get so randy on buses.* Christ almighty.

She said, "Feel my heart, Chip," and she took my hand and placed it on her left breast. "Can you feel it?"

I couldn't feel her heart beat, perhaps because my own had suddenly grown so loud. I could certainly feel her breast, though. I felt it through the thicknesses of sweater and bra, felt the nipple poking against my palm.

I cupped her breast, stroked with my fingers. It was as warm and soft as a little bird. I kept the little bird in my hand and dreamed of giving her two in the bush.

Our mouths found one another. She tasted of cigarettes. I don't like to smoke but I like that taste on a girl's mouth. We slid into an all-out kiss right off the bat. She was very goddamned good at kissing. We kissed for miles, and I held her breast as if I was afraid it would fly away if I let it go. I wasn't about to take any chances.

When we broke the kiss she sagged back in her seat with her eyes closed and her jaw slack. Her breathing was really ragged. I was a little shook up myself but she was way out ahead of me.

Finally she said, "Get my coat, Chip."

"You can't leave now. I mean, the least you have to do is wait until the bus stops."

"*Leave*? Who's leaving?"

"Not me. I thought you wanted your coat."

She sighed and tsssted at me. "Don't you have no sense?" she whispered. "To put over us. To neck under. So nobody sees us."

"Oh."

"Because I'm not about to stop now. Chip, I told you how I get on buses, and then reading that scene with them . . . and then you messing around with me, I mean I'm not about to stop now."

"Fine by me."

"Now fetch my coat."

55

I fetched her coat and draped it over us. While I was getting it I checked out the other people in the area. If any of them were checking us out in return they were doing a good job of hiding it. The seats across the aisle were empty, and most of our other neighbors were asleep.

As soon as I was seated beside her she grabbed my hand and tucked it up under her mini skirt. She was wearing panties. Very moist panties.

I said, "Willie Em—"

"Shhhh!" she whispered. "No more talking, Chip. Oh, Lord have mercy, I'm so hot I could *burn*! But don't talk, don't say anything. Just get me off. God, please get me *off*—"

The thing is, she kept getting off and climbing right back on again. There was only so much we could do. I played with her and that was about the extent of it. She was unbelievably responsive. Each orgasm just seemed to make her that much more anxious for the next one.

This went on for maybe half an hour, and I could see where it was destined to go on all the way to Bordentown unless I happened to run out of fingers somewhere along the way.

And I was going to get off the bus in Borden-town with testicles the size of basketballs, and they were going to hurt like hell, and that was just too damned bad because I had already decided it was worth it.

Maybe she wasn't the only one who got horny on buses. Maybe it was the other people around, or maybe it was the build-up and letdown I'd gotten earlier from Mary Beth, or maybe it was just Willamina Emily Weeks herself, but whatever it was, it was worth six Waterloos and an Armageddon. I mean it was very goddamned exciting, believe me.

God knows how many little orgasms she had. I couldn't keep score. But she finally got the big one and collapsed like a tubercular lung.

In less than two minutes we pulled off the highway and stopped for a ten-minute rest break in Erewhon, North Carolina.

I swear she planned it that way.

She said, "Get my suitcase down, Chip. And put your jacket over those two seats across the aisle, and leave my coat here. And when we come back you sit over there and

57

sort of take up both seats until the bus moves.
So no one sits across from us, you hear?"

I heard and I did. I didn't know why she
wanted her suitcase, or why we had to get off
the bus and back on again, or any of those
things, really. I would have understood the
bit about the coats even if she hadn't explained it to me, although I'll admit I
wouldn't have thought of it on my own, not
just then.

But I wasn't going to bug her about any of
this. I mean, it was pretty obvious this wasn't
the first time she ever got randy on a bus,
and it wasn't the first time she ever decided
to do anything about it. This bus fetish was
something she had indulged in before. And
probably often. Which was why she sat down
next to me to begin with. And why she
wanted the window seat—partly so that we
could bump bottoms while changing places,
and partly because she would be better
shielded from observation if she sat away
from the aisle.

I didn't really want to get off the bus and
back on again. Walking presented certain lo-
gistical problems that would be even more
obvious to spectators if I had to leave my

jacket on the bus. But I got off and I forced myself to drink a Coke and munch a pack of those peanut butter and cheese things. I waited until she emerged from the ladies' room and got on board the bus before I followed her. She put her suitcase on the seat beside her so that no one could sit there, and I sprawled over the two opposite seats and looked as unkempt as possible so that no one would want to sit next to me. She waited until the bus was back on the highway before giving me a nod, and I came over and put her suitcase overhead and sat down next to her.

We huddled together under her coat and kissed briefly. Then I said, "Why the suitcase?"

"Can't you guess?"

The only thing that had occurred to me was that she wanted to put her diaphragm on, but I couldn't believe that. This was a bus, after all, and it wasn't particularly comfortable or roomy even if all you wanted to do was sit in it. I know people screw in the most unlikely places, but only midgets and contortionists could possibly do it on a bus.

I had already decided that the best I could hope for was to shoot in my pants, if you'll forgive me for being crude about it. (I can't really think of any other way to say it.) And I wasn't all that sure I wanted to do that. I don't suppose I really cared about getting off myself. I just wanted to go on thrilling Willie Em.

"No," I said, "I can't guess."

"Did that old suitcase feel heavier this time?"

"No."

"It was, though."

"It was?"

She grinned impishly. "Something in it that wasn't in it before."

What? A roll of toilet paper? A Coke? What?

"What?"

"You have to find out for yourself. But I'll bet you appreciate the change."

"I think you lost me."

"Why, I surely hope not! Now why don't you shut your mouth and start loving me up instead of asking all those questions?"

I had no argument there. I kissed her and put a hand on her breast. It felt softer than ever. I petted it and light dawned.

"Oh."

"Uh-huh. And that's just the half of it."

I could guess the other half, but I sent my hand on an expedition to make sure. I slipped it under her skirt and there were no panties there. The panties, like the bra, were currently in her suitcase.

I hope she wrung them out first.

It certainly did make things easier. We snuggled under her coat and unbuttoned her cardigan and pulled her skirt all the way up, and all of sudden there was a lot more to do. She had wonderfully soft skin and nice firm little breasts. The perfume she was wearing mixed nicely with the musk of her.

I was going to put down a whole description of just what we did over the next couple of hours, but I've been thinking about it and I decided the hell with it. Partly because I think that would just be too much sex. And despite what Mr. Fultz said, I think there is such a thing as too much sex.

Because when all you have is a description of what happened, who did what and where and how and all of that, then all you've got is the kind of book Willie Em was reading, *The Swinging Swappers* or *The Swapping Swingers*. And that sort of thing may be exciting in small doses, but it's also pretty disgusting, actually.

What's important, really, is what it was like and where everybody's head was at while it was going on, or otherwise it's just bodies with no people attached to them. And anyway we kept on like this for a couple of hours, and I couldn't honestly remember the whole thing piece by piece. It would be easy enough to fake it and get the tone right the same way I fake some of the dialogue because I can't actually remember every stupid conversation I ever had word for word. Let's just say that I kept doing things to her and she kept enjoying them and let's let it go at that. I figure that if all you wanted in the way of a book was something to get off with you would have stopped reading before now and gone on to the swinging switching swapping swill.

Three times in the course of all this I took her hand and put it on me. Twice she gave a little squeeze and murmured *"Later."* The third time she repeated this and added, "When it gets dark, Chip."

You know, I wonder how often she did this.

I mean, she had the whole thing choreographed, for Pete's sake. Sometimes when I think about her I picture her spending her entire life riding north and south on Greyhound buses. Maybe her aunt doesn't even *have* pleurisy. Maybe she doesn't even have an *aunt*. Maybe Greyhound gives her a commuter's rate. Maybe they let her ride free because it's such great public relations for them. Maybe—

When it got dark, I didn't even have to reach for her hand. It came over of its own accord and quickly found what it was looking for. She gave a few affectionate squeezes, worked a zipper, reached in, and brought her hand quickly back out again.

She put her lips to my ear and whispered, "Why don't you go to the lavatory and take off your shorts?"

I guess I should have done this at the rest stop. God knows it would have been a lot easier. The lavatory wasn't really spacious enough to change clothes in. It was barely big enough to take a leak in, actually.

I came back with my shorts in my pocket and got under the coat again. Then she decided we should change places, with me sitting in the window seat and her on the outside, and somehow we managed to do this without getting out from under the coat. Don't ask me how.

"Poor old Chip," she murmured. "Getting me off about a hundred times"—at the very least, I thought—"and you never getting off once your own self. But we'll fix that."

And I sat there with her head in my lap and my hand bunched up in all that yellow hair and she fixed everything in the world. She fixed things that weren't even broken.

Wow.

Afterward, while I waited for the top of my skull to come back down where it belonged, she nestled her sweet and talented little head on my shoulder. After a while she said, "Happy?"

"Mmmmm."

"You like being loved up that way?"

"Mmmmm."

"They tell me girls up North don't like to do that. Damned if I know why. First time I did that I wasn't but fourteen years old and at a drive-in movie and too dumb to know about keeping my teeth out of the way, and the good old boy I was with was too dumb to tell me." She giggled. "You like that kind of loving, you're gonna enjoy yourself down South. Southern girls are decent, see. And they know the one thing that's not decent is getting pregnant before you're married, and another thing they know is no girl ever got a big belly from it."

From her tone of voice she could have been talking about crop rotation and soil erosion. It was really weird.

I said, "The purity of Southern womanhood."

"You better believe it. Next Southern girl you meet and get friendly with, you tell her to try it with a mouthful of warm water. Of course you couldn't do that on a bus."

"The Waterloo," I said.

"You know about that?"

"Uh-huh."

"They know about that up North?"

"Not exactly."

"You ever have it done?"

"Not exactly."

"What do you mean, 'Not exactly'?"

"It's hard to explain."

"Well—?"

"I read about it."

"In a *book*?"

"Uh-huh."

"Like the kind of book I was reading before? One of those randy books?"

"More or less."

"Lordy," she said. "I'll usually get a book like that to read if, oh, if I happen to have to take a long trip on a bus." I could believe it. "I've read my share of them, I guess. Never read anything about the Waterloo in any old book."

"Maybe it was written by a Southern girl," I suggested.

"No maybe about it. It must have been."

"Maybe a girl from Tennessee."

"Georgia," she said.

FOUR

THE BUS STATION IN BORDENTOWN WAS just an Atlantic gas station that sold bus tickets. They had a Coke machine, but I passed it up. I was down to about two and a half dollars and I didn't know where I was going to get a room, or how much it would cost. I figured the Y was the best bet, and I asked an old guy at the station how to get to it.

He scratched his head and said, "Why?"

"Because I need a place to stay."

"But you asked—"

"The Y," I said. He was still puzzled. "The YMCA," I said.

"Oh, the YMCA. Let me just think. I believe

67

they have one over to Savolia, but I couldn't say for sure."

"How far is that?"

"Oh, I guess I'd put it at twenty-eight miles. Say thirty at the outside."

There was a hotel in Bordentown, he told me. It was called the Bordentown Hotel, which seemed logical enough, and it was on Main Street, which wasn't all that much of a surprise either. Salesmen would stay there, if they had to be in Bordentown overnight, and if they wanted to save money, because those motels over on the highway all ranged from eight to twelve dollars a room, whereas you could stay at the hotel for five dollars, or seven-fifty with a private bath. And then there were some single people who lived there year-round, widowers for the most part, and they paid by the month, which made it considerably cheaper.

"Of course you wouldn't be wanting to spend a month in Bordentown," he said.

I had the feeling he might be right. Anyway, I couldn't afford to pay by the month. I couldn't even afford to pay by the night. I asked if there were any less expensive places. He said there were some women who took in tourists for two or three dollars a night, but it was too late to go knocking on their doors.

"How would it be if I slept in the back here?" I suggested. "It would just be for tonight."

"Company wouldn't allow that."

I said I wouldn't tell them if he didn't, but he didn't even bother answering that. He didn't get exactly hostile, just sort of turned away. I had the feeling that he didn't see much point in wasting any more time on me, and I could understand his point of view.

I must have spent half an hour walking through the main part of town, and that was enough to cover it pretty thoroughly. There really wasn't a lot there. It was about then that I started wondering if coming to Bordentown might not have been something of a mistake. Of course, it was the middle of the night. You couldn't really expect a small town to be lit up like Times Square.

Until now, though, I had been very much into the idea of going to Bordentown. The weirdness of it, finding the bus ticket and using it, had a special beauty of its own. In the normal course of things I might have spent the last few hours of the bus trip thinking about what I would do after I got off the bus, making plans and working things out in my mind. But you know how I spent the last few hours of the bus trip. I spent the last few hours of the bus trip with Willie Em, and the company of Willie Em tends to make one live very much in the Now.

As a matter of fact, the *memory* of Willie Em tends to make one live very much in the Past, and while I walked around downtown Bordentown, such as it was, I found myself thinking as much about her as about my future. I couldn't really get into anything like long-term planning at all. Just short-term goals, like getting a place to sleep and finding some kind of job, were the only things I could really handle.

The place to sleep was the hard part. At that hour it seemed impossible. The only place I could go was the hotel, and I couldn't afford it. If I had only had a suitcase it would have been all right, because I could tell them I was staying for a week, and if things went well I would have enough money at the end of the week to pay what I owed. On the other hand, if things went badly I could leave them the suitcase at the end of the week and go someplace else, and all that would mean was that I could never go back to Bordentown again, which didn't sound that terrible anyway.

No suitcase, though. Nothing but the clothes on my back, which had seen cleaner days. So any hotel would be sure to ask for cash in advance. The fact that I was poor but honest wouldn't help. They'd rather have someone who's rich but crooked.

It's funny how problems solve themselves, though, when you just let things happen. I had more or less resigned myself to finding some diner and sitting up drinking coffee until morning, at which time I could get some old lady to rent me a room that I could afford, when I got a place to sleep that didn't cost me a dime.

The Bordentown Jail.

I was walking along when this car pulled up and a voice said, "Git over here, boy." And when I got over there I knew who the guy was without him saying another word. I recognized him right away from all those Dodge commercials.

He never did advise me of my rights, but I

don't guess he had to because he never exactly arrested me, either. He just told me to get in the car with him, and he drove over to a little concrete block building a few blocks from where he picked me up, and he asked me a lot of questions and took my fingerprints and put me in a cell. He took my belt and my shoelaces and my comb. I was getting sick of losing combs, and I hadn't been eating much lately and my pants, without the belt, tended to fall down a lot. But I didn't complain.

I didn't complain about any of this, actually. I was at a tremendous psychological disadvantage, especially when he made me empty my pockets and I had to take out that pair of undershorts and put them on the desk. Maybe some people can do that without feeling stupid. Not me.

He said, "No identification, no visible means of support, no clothing. You say you're from New York, boy? What you think you're doing here?"

I don't remember what I said.

"You an agitator? Come down to make trouble? Or a runaway? You wanted up North? Get your prints and description to

72

Washington and see if there isn't somebody looking for you."

There was something about the way the cell door closed that left me feeling it would never open again. I walked around the cell, which was a lot like walking around Bordentown except that it didn't take quite so long. There was a kind of a toilet, which I'm just as glad I didn't have to use, and a corn husk mattress that was more comfortable than it looked.

During the summer some of my fellow apple-knockers had told me stories about Southern jails. About getting caught in a speed trap and being fined the amount they had on them, and then winding up on the chain gang on a vagrancy charge because they didn't have any money. About trying to hitch-hike through Georgia and getting sentenced to three months of chopping weeds with a road crew.

I remembered all this now, and I really didn't think I was going to get much sleep. But I must have been more exhausted than I realized.

I woke up when the sun came through the bars. I just lay there for about an hour before the Sheriff turned up, trying to put together pieces of a story that would keep me off the chain gang.

At first I decided to tell him the truth. I must have read a hundred murder stories where some poor idiot is suspected of a crime, and if he had just played things absolutely straight from the beginning it would have worked out with no trouble, but instead he tells one little lie or holds something back and gets in deeper trouble, until he has to go out and find the real killer himself. Of course, if he played things absolutely straight there wouldn't have been any book, so I can understand why writers do it that way, but the moral always seemed to be that the truth shall make you free.

But it seemed to me that the truth in my case would make me very much unfree. In the first place, nobody was going to believe it. If I said I found a wallet that somebody had already stolen, anyone with half a brain would decide that I had stolen it. And if I said I came to Bordentown because I had a ticket that made it a toss-up between Bordentown and Boston, and Bordentown was warmer, and I didn't want to spit in the face of destiny,

and how one Mary Beth could lead to another, well, all that would do was keep me
off the chain gang and land me in the insane asylum.

The trouble with the truth was that it just
didn't sound true enough. And by the time
he unlocked my cell door and came on in, I
had thought up a few ways to improve it.

"Well, now," he said. "I guess you ain't
precisely Johnny Dillinger after all. Your fingerprints didn't ring any bells and nobody up
in Washington got too excited about your
description."

I had been a little worried that I might still
be wanted in Indiana for statutory rape, but
I guess that got straightened out somewhere
along the way. I knew my fingerprints had
never gotten on file.

(Until now.)

"But that seems to make you what they call
an unknown quantity, boy." He clucked his
tongue. "Chip Harrison. That some kind of
a nickname?"

"It's my real name."

"Your folks handed you that, did they?
Where are they now?"

"They were killed in an auto crash a little over a year ago."

"Any other kinfolk?"

"None."

"And no way on earth to prove you're who you say you are. No identification at all."

"My wallet was stolen. In New York."

He looked at me.

"They got my wallet and my suitcase. I was on my way to Florida. To Miami, I couldn't stand it in New York with the weather and the kind of people you meet up there. I had my ticket bought and I was on my way to the bus station when they jumped me."

"Jumped you?"

"Three big buck niggers," I said. "One of them held a razor to my throat. I think you can still see the nick. Then one of the others hit me a few times in the stomach. They got my watch and my wallet and my suitcase, they even got the change out of my pocket. I had the ticket in my shoe."

"That was good thinking," he said. "You go to the police?"

"In New York? What good would that do?"

"I hear tell it's another country up there."

"More like another world. If you tell those

New York police you've been robbed, they act like you're wasting their time." Which was true enough, incidentally. When I had a place in the East Village, somebody kicked the door in one day and robbed me, which was actually one big reason why I didn't have anything but the clothes on my back. I wasn't there at the time, and there had never been anyone holding a razor to my throat, but you can see that the story had elements of truth to it. It was sort of a matter of arranging the truth so that it made sense.

"So all I had was the ticket," I went on. "I had sixty-two dollars left after I bought my ticket, but they got it when they got the wallet. I figured it would be plenty to keep me going until I found work in Miami. A fellow was telling me there were plenty of jobs down there. At those hotels."

"That the kind of work you did in New York?"

"No, I was bussing tables in a cafeteria." I actually did that for a day once, in a cafeteria on Second Avenue. That job ended when I dropped a tray. They took it for granted that you would drop a tray now and then, but not on a customer. "But from what I heard you didn't need much experience to hire on as a bellhop or something."

He was nodding. He didn't really look like that Dodge commercial anymore.

"After they robbed me," I said, "I didn't know what to do. I just knew I had to get out of New York."

"No place for a white man."

"That's the truth," I said. "Dope addicts and niggers and long-haired radicals and I don't know what else. And being robbed and all, I just wanted to get away from there. But I didn't want to go to Miami with no money at all. I figured I'd starve before I got settled. So I worked out how much money I would need and traded my ticket so that I could get as close as possible to Miami and still have a few dollars left to live on."

"And that's how you picked Bordentown. I was wondering about that."

"I guess it would have been better to stop further north. In North Carolina, say, because that would have left me with more money. But I wanted to get as far as I could, and anyway my mother was from South Carolina originally—"

"Is that a fact?"

"She was born in Charleston. Her maiden name was Ryder. But there's no family left now."

"I didn't think you seemed like the typical Yankee."

"Well, I've always lived in the North. But I never felt, you know, that it was really home to me."

We went on like this for a while, and he got less and less like that Dodge commercial and I got more and more South Carolina into my voice. I didn't want to get carried away and lay it on too thick, but as long as it was going over well I figured it was worth staying with. He wanted to know about my plans. I said I would just try to find work in Bordentown. There weren't many jobs, he said. Ever since the space people closed their operations in Savolia, jobs were tight all over the area. Especially in the winter, when there was no farm work to speak of. I said I was willing to do just about anything, and as soon as I had money saved I could go down to Miami.

"Don't want to go anywhere without some identification," he said. "You'd get the same reception anywhere. First police officer who sets eyes on you wouldn't have no choice but to lock you up. I suspect you can write away for certain things. Driver's license, for example."

"I never had one."

"Draft card, for certain. This day and age you don't want to go anywhere without a draft card."

"I'm only seventeen," I said. On my eighteenth birthday I had decided that it wouldn't hurt to stay seventeen as long as possible. It seemed to me that if you didn't get around to registering for the draft you wouldn't have to make any Big Decision as to whether or not you would burn your draft card.

"Need a social security card," he said. "You must of had one, I guess. Recollect the number?"

I didn't.

"Easier to go ahead and get a new one, then. You try writing to them for a replacement and those fellows in Washington, they'll be a year getting back to you. I could tell you stories about those people up there. What else you'll need is a Sheriff's ID Card. I'll fix you up with one of those. At least we can do that without going through a passel of red tape. You just apply for a social security card down to the courthouse, and on the form you put that you never had one before. That's the easiest way to go about it. Not entirely legal, but in police work you learn that there's laws and there's laws. Know what I mean?"

"Laws to help people and laws to get in people's way?"

"I guess you understand my meaning, boy." He looked at me and I looked back at him, deciding that he was a pretty nice guy. He clucked his tongue again. "Reckon you could do with a bath and a change of clothes," he said. "Or with running what clothes you got through the washing machine. The wife can do that while you're in the tub." I almost said I didn't have a wife. Then I realized we were talking about his wife, and his washing machine, and his tub.

"Like to had me wondering when you pulled those drawers out of your pocket last night. I sat up wondering what kind of damned fool pervert carries his underwear in his pocket. Guess they must of been chafing you some on that bus ride. How long were you on that bus?"

"On to forty hours."

He clucked again. "And eating in those

greasy diners, were you? Fifty cents for a hamburger sandwich and you have to hunt for the meat, and fifteen cents for coffee that's not but brown water. Never had a real Southern breakfast up there, did you?"

"No."

"Grits and eggs and fries and sausage and coffee that the spoon stands up in? I guess they don't know how to eat up there. What's that Northern food like?"

I didn't mention brown rice. "Like a machine made it," I said.

"You come on now," he said, beaming. He led me out of the cell. "I'll just get you set with a sheriff's card, and then we'll take a run over to my home and see if you got the kind of appetite that would have made your mother proud. Look at the way those pants are falling off of you. I swear the wife's gone take one look at you and run straight for the kitchen. Nothing brings out her cooking like someone who looks like he could profit from it." He patted his belly, of which there was quite a lot. "She feels guilty, feeding me. But you'll be a real challenge to her."

I said, "This is awfully nice of you," or something like that.

"Oh, just put it down to Southern hospitality," he said, grinning. "We don't cotton to everybody. But we take care of our own kind, boy."

FIVE

BY THE END OF THE WEEK I HAD A SHER-
iff's ID Card, a social security card, and a
South Carolina driver's license. I also had two
jobs, one of which paid me fifteen dollars a
week and my lunches, and the other of which
brought in five dollars a week, breakfasts,
dinners, and a room of my own. Sheriff Tyles
fixed me up with the license and one of the
jobs, and his wife Minnie got me the other
one.

(I had to take a road test for the license. I
had never done much in the way of driving,
and I don't know that I had any natural talent
for it, but the test was no great problem.
When you take the test in the official sheriff's

car, there aren't a hell of a lot of inspectors who are likely to fail you. I didn't hit anybody, so I passed.)

Minnie Tyles took to me right off. I hadn't been that confident she would be thrilled when her husband brought me home. Forty hours on a bus and a night in a jail cell hadn't improved my appearance that much. But when we walked in the door he boomed out, "Minnie, this here boy hasn't had a decent meal in three days and his mother was a Charleston Ryder." I don't know which part of the sentence went over the heaviest. I was a little lost myself, and for a minute there I thought he was saying that my mother was a member of some South Carolina version of the Hell's Angels.

I had about four meals, and I had them all at once. And then I had a bath while my clothes washed and dried, and then I had a big piece of pie and another couple of cups of coffee. The more I ate the happier that woman got. It was really something to watch.

"Of course he'll sleep here until he finds some place," she told the Sheriff. "Won't be any trouble to fix up the spare room for him." I said something about not wanting to im-

pose, and they both acted as though they
hadn't heard me, which was fine with me.

The job situation didn't look very promis-
ing. There wasn't much available, and most
of the high school kids left town when they
graduated, unless their fathers had businesses
for them to go into. I spent a couple of days
looking for work and couldn't get anywhere.
"I couldn't ask you to work for what-all I can
afford to pay you," one shopkeeper said.
"Easier to hire a nigger for fifty cents an hour,
and I wouldn't let you work for that kind of
wages even if you said you would. And with
business the way it is I couldn't pay you
more."

Then Minnie came up with something. "Now
I'll tell you right off it isn't so much of a job,"
she said. "But Reverend Lathrop has been
poorly lately that's at the church we go to,
and with his wife gone two years in May it's
all he can do to look after himself. Lucille
that's his daughter cooks his meals for him
and does the cleaning, what she can keep up
with; some of the women from the church do
his ironing and all, but if there was someone
who would come in a few hours a day, be-

cause with it being an old house and all and things always breaking down, and the yard to keep up and the trash to be taken out, and what with one thing or another, and him getting along in years, he was twenty years older than Helen that was his wife, and her dying first, and Lucille still in school so that she has to run home and cook his dinner for him and then back to school again—"

It wasn't very much work. The main reason that Rev. Lathrop was poorly was that he did in a quart of corn whiskey every day. This tended to limit his movements, and he spent most of his time sitting in the back parlor with a bottle and a glass listening to the radio. I did things like shoveling ashes out of the coal furnace and taking out the trash (and burying the empty liquor bottles under the rest of the garbage). I would get there around ten in the morning, by which time Lucille was off at school and her father was already at work on the daily bottle. She came home at noon and fixed dinner for us, and then I did things like trimming shrubbery and replacing frayed lamp cords and repainting the upstairs bathroom, sort of doing all the repairs and maintenance work that tends to get neglected when you knock off a quart a day. How late I stayed depended on whether or not Lucille came straight home from school. She was a cheerleader, and if there was a basketball game or a practice session scheduled she wouldn't get home until five or six. No one ever exactly spelled it out, but the idea was that Rev. Lathrop shouldn't be left alone if there was a way to avoid it. I don't know what they were worried about. I never saw him get off that chair. Lucille used to bring his dinner to him, and he ate between drinks. He had a pretty good appetite for someone who drank that much, but he never really paid attention to his food, just ate it because it was there. I had the feeling that if she skipped his dinner he wouldn't notice it.

He didn't bother me, though. He would look at me if I was in the room, and now and then he would quote scripture, but if I spoke he never gave any sign that he had heard, so before long I got out of the habit of talking to him. Once I had an insane urge to polish his bald head along with the furniture, just to see what would happen. Of course I didn't, but I'm not sure he would have noticed.

One Sunday I let Minnie take me to hear

him preach a sermon. The Sheriff never went to church, but Minnie went religiously. She introduced me to all her friends, which took in most of the congregation, and told everybody my mother was a Charleston Ryder. (Actually my mother's maiden name was Leigh, which was where my first name came from, but that sounded too Southern to be true. And she was from Lawrence, Kansas, and I think her grandparents ran a way station of the Underground Railway for runaway slaves headed north. I don't think that would have gone over as well with this crowd.)

The one time I heard him preach, I had trouble believing it was the same vegetable who spent the other six days of the week in the back parlor. He stood straight and tall and had a great deal of presence. The sermon itself wasn't designed to make you think a whole hell of a lot. He came out against sin, creeping socialism, federal intervention, drinking, gambling, and sins of the flesh, without getting too specific on any of these points. I won't say I enjoyed it, but I was really proud of him the way he stayed on top of things. I was sure he would fall over or forget what he was talking about, but he never once dropped the ball. He was pretty impressive.

When I finished up at the Lathrop house, sometimes I would drop over to the station and talk with the Sheriff, and about twice a week I would get invited home for dinner. Or I might see a movie. There was one movie house in town and they changed the bill three times a week, and even so the movie was usually one I had seen four or five years ago. The theater was always close to empty, and whether or not they had an afternoon show depended on how many people showed up. Mr. Crewe wouldn't run the projector unless he had at least ten people in the audience.

He was one of the people I'd tried to hit for a job. I never heard a man laugh louder. "Why, if I paid *myself* a salary," he said, "I'd go broke tomorrow. I'd have to close."

Then, after the movie, or instead of the movie, I would sometimes stop for a cup of coffee at a diner. The coffee wasn't sensational but one of the waitresses was, and I liked to talk to her. She had told me that she wouldn't go out with me because her boy friend was in Vietnam, and I was only seventeen and she was nineteen and she didn't go with boys younger than herself. I figured sooner or later she would change her mind, and even if she didn't the coffee wasn't that godawful.

Then I would walk about a mile out of town, or get a lift if I had had supper with the Sheriff and Minnie. There was a place there on one of the country roads called the Lighthouse, where I had a room and got my morning and evening meals.

"It's not a job with a future," Sheriff Tyles said, "but you could do worse. It puts a roof over your head and a few dollars in your pocket and it's good experience if you ever want to go into law enforcement. Old Geraldine runs a decent place. You won't find water in the liquor and you'll never hear of a customer getting rolled, not even one from out of the state which you would expect. Now and then a fight will get out of hand and there'll be a certain amount of cutting, but you always have that when you have men and whiskey. Hasn't been anybody killed there in onto four years, and that was Johnny Piersall that everybody was surprised he lasted that long. If there was ever a boy looking to get killed, that was Johnny Piersall.

"And Geraldine has a doctor in once a week, and everything is clean and decent. So for the most part all you have to do is be there. You'll be a deputy in case you have to go so far as to make an arrest, but I doubt that'll happen at all. You might have to stop a fight now and then if it gets too ornery, or you might have to hit some old boy upside the head for abusing one of the girls. But being there is the main thing, and the less you have to do the more Geraldine will like it. It's like a life insurance policy, there's never yet been anybody complaining that he's not getting sufficient use out of it."

So that was my job. From around nine at night until around four in the morning, with time for a nap in the early evening unless something came up and they had to call me. At the Lighthouse, owned and operated by Geraldine Simms.

There are, as Sheriff Tyles and I had agreed, laws and laws. Laws to help people and laws to get in people's way. I guess I had always had more or less that attitude myself, and maybe more of it when you consider my parents' occupation and my own work as a termite salesman. (Not that I actually sold termites.)

Even so, I have to admit that the job came as a surprise to me. I'd already had a lot of unusual jobs, and in fact I had gotten to the point where I took it for granted that I would go on having unusual jobs. I always figured that sooner or later I would find what I had been looking for all along, which is to say a Job With A Future, but that never seemed to be the kind of job I got and I was beginning to see a pattern developing.

But I never expected to be employed as a Deputy Sheriff in a South Carolina whorehouse.

I just never expected it.

SIX

GERALDINE SHOOK HER HEAD. "YOU'RE in trouble now, Chip."

"I am?"

"Bad trouble."

"I don't see it."

Her hand, thin with a tracing of blue veins, moved quickly and decisively. She lifted a pawn of mine, set her bishop in its place.

"Check," she said.

"Oh."

"Think it out if you want, but I can speed it up for you. If you play King takes Bishop, I play Queen to King Eight—Checkmate. If you play King to Bishop One, I play Bishop takes Queen."

I looked at the board for a minute, and she was right. She generally was. I nodded slowly.

"You resign?"

"Uh-huh."

"Want another game?"

"Not right now. I have a feeling I'm never going to learn this game."

"You're getting better."

"I can't keep my mind on it the way you can, that's the thing. I used to play in New York and I would win most of the time because I could see a move or so in advance, and that was better than the guys I played against. I even thought I was pretty good, because of generally winning."

"You're not so bad."

"Thanks," I said. I gathered the pieces and put them back in the cigar box. We were in the barroom, and there were three beer-drinkers in the bar. Geraldine went to see if they wanted refills. They didn't. It was around eleven, the middle of the week, and business couldn't have been much slower. Geraldine came back with a cold Coke for me and her usual glass of banana liqueur.

We talked about this and that, and then

Geraldine was starting to say, "That tobacco farmer's been a long time with Claureen," when I looked up and Claureen was standing there in a pink wrapper and house slippers.

She said, "Chip? Could you come on up for a minute?"

"Trouble?"

"Just that he's asleep and I can't wake him and I was afraid if I did wake him and he woke up nasty like they will sometimes—"

"He's not a regular," Geraldine said. "This is his first time." This meant he wasn't a treasured customer, so if it would simplify things to beat his brains in I should just go ahead and do it.

I got to my feet. Geraldine said something about the kind of men who fall asleep the minute they finish. Claureen took my hand and we walked to the stairs.

On the staircase she said, "It's not like she said."

"What isn't?"

"I declare it's too embarrassing to say. He didn't fall asleep after. He fell asleep while."

"While what?"

"What do you think?"

"Oh. Too much to drink, probably."

"No, that's not it. I know when they can't because they been drinking. It's not he can't. Oh, you'll see what I mean."

In her room I saw what she meant. The tobacco farmer was stretched out on his back with his eyes closed and his arms at his sides. He had his socks and shoes on and nothing else.

"You see how he is, Chip? He's still hard."

"Uh, yeah. So he is."

"He just sprawled out like that and I started doing him, you know, and he got like that right away. Just lying still like that, and hard as a bar of iron. And I did him and did him and did him and nothing happened. And I got to thinking, all right, you silly old son of a bitch, just how long is it gone take before you get where you're going? But I just kept on and then I wasn't even thinking about what I was doing, I thought about getting my hair done and I don't know what-all, and the time just went on by—"

"Geraldine was saying he was taking a long time."

"—and finally I thought maybe he was one of those who couldn't finish that way, and I looked up to ask him, and he was like you see him, and I talked to him, and nothing; he was dead to the world."

"You tried to wake him?"

"A little. I was scared, you know, to try too much."

I went over and put a hand on the man's shoulder. I gave him a shake.

Nothing happened.

"I even put water on his face," Claureen said.

"No reaction?"

"Nothing."

"I wonder if he's dead."

She grabbed my arm. "Oh, Holy Jesus! Chip, don't you even go and *say* a thing like that!"

"Did you check?"

"No, but—"

"Because it's possible, you know."

"Would it stay like that after you were dead?"

"I don't know."

"What a horrible thing!"

"I don't know. If you gotta go—"

"Oh, Mother of Pearl," she said. She was trembling. "Imagine me doing that to a dead man. Oh, I'm just shaking fit to die myself!"

I picked up his wrist and looked around for his pulse. It took me a little while, but ultimately I found what I was looking for and told Claureen she wasn't a murderess.

"I thought I Frenched him to death," she said. "Oh, mercy."

"You may have Frenched him into a coma," I told her. "His pulse is there but it's very slow. It's as if he was in some kind of hypnotic trance."

"I hypnotized him? I didn't say anything like, 'Look into my eyes,' or any of that. All I did was—"

"I know what you did," I said, quickly. "Maybe I'd better tell Geraldine to call the doctor."

"At this hour?"

"I don't know what'll happen if we wait until morning. Suppose he comes to in the middle of the night? With nobody around?" I put my ear to his face. "Or suppose he *does* die, for that matter. He's breathing, but it's so faint you wouldn't believe it."

"What'll we do?"

"Maybe an orgasm would wake him."

"That's what I *tried*, Chip. That's what took

so long. I did everything I could think of. Even the vibrator."

"And nothing worked?"

"Nothing. If it worked, he wouldn't be here."

"That's a point."

"What'll we do?"

"I'm going to tell Geraldine."

"She'll kill me," Claureen said.

"Don't be ridiculous. It's not your fault."

I went downstairs and told Geraldine what the problem was. Rita was sitting with her at the time. There were just the two girls there during the week, Rita and Claureen. They both had rooms upstairs that they slept in after working hours. On weekends or particularly busy nights another girl would work the busy hours, usually Jo Lee or Marguerite.

Rita just stared while I was talking. "I never heard the like," she said.

"I have," Geraldine said. "Never saw it, but heard of it. Heard of men overdosing with sleeping pills and then going with a girl, and they never wake up afterward, but that's something else because they don't stay hard like that. But I've heard of this, too. What you have to do is get their rocks off and then they wake up."

"Claureen hasn't been able to," I said. "And she tried everything."

"Don't even ask me," Rita said.

"Oh, I won't." Geraldine thought for a moment.

"Claureen's young," she said, and went silent again. Then she said, "God damn it to hell, you just never get to retire in this business. You think you're retired and you find out you're not. God damn it to hell."

She got up and went to the stairs. Rita and I sat and looked at each other.

I said, "I never heard her swear before."

"Neither did I. And I've been here for almost three years. Geraldine wouldn't say shit if she had a mouthful. I can't believe it, Chip."

"What happens now?"

"I don't know."

What happened was that Claureen came downstairs. She was wearing a dress and shoes instead of the wrapper and slippers. We stared at her. She came over and sat down at our table.

"She cursed," she said, hollowly. "Geraldine cursed."

"Did she curse *you*, honey?"

She shook her head. "She just cursed generally, like. She said, 'God damn it to hell.' "

"She said it down here. Twice."

"And then she told me to put a dress on and come downstairs. I didn't want to just go and leave her there with that, uh, with *him*, and I said I don't know what-all, and she just turned and looked at me. And I just put on the dress and the shoes and I came down here."

"You look so pale, girl."

"Look at how I'm shaking—"

Rita said, "Was she doin' anything?"

"What do you mean?"

"With that farmer."

"Oh. She made me leave the room. She wouldn't even look at him until I left the room, and then—"

"What?"

"She locked the door. You know what she always said, that you never lock the door unless you-all are alone in the room. Geraldine locked the door."

I started to say something, then stopped. The girls saw the expression on my face and followed my eyes to the staircase. The tobacco farmer was coming down it, neatly dressed, an absolutely blank look in his eyes. He came down and he walked out and the door closed behind him.

Maybe two minutes later Geraldine came down. She passed our table without a glance and drew a couple of beers for the drinkers at the bar. One of them said something and she joked back with them the way she always did. Then she came back to our table.

For the longest time in the world nobody said anything. It was really weird. We were all waiting for Geraldine to talk up, and she was off in some other world.

Finally she said, "You never really retire. You just can't, want to or not."

Claureen or Rita said, "What happened?"

"He came and went. Or he'd be there still, saluting the ceiling."

Claureen or Rita said, "But what did you—"

There was a pause on the order of the Grand Canyon during which a whole load of expressions flashed over Geraldine's face. You couldn't really read any of them because none of them were there long enough.

Then all at once her whole face smiled. I can't remember ever seeing a smile like that one before or since, and certainly not from Geraldine. A sour grin was more her usual speed. But this smile was the real thing, with lights going on and everything.

And she said, "I'm not going to tell you."

And she never did.

That was a whole lot more excitement than we usually had. Most of the time nothing much happened. You know, if someone had told me I was going to be a Deputy Sheriff in a South Carolina whorehouse I would have thought he was crazy, but if he'd gone on to tell me I'd be generally bored with the job I would have *known* he was crazy. I mean, what could be boring about it?

The thing is, there wasn't much to do. Five days a week there wasn't much for any of us to do, and it was a big night if Claureen and Rita turned half a dozen tricks between them. Fridays and Saturdays were busier, particularly Saturdays, when the workers drew their pay and the farmers came into town to do their trading. I never tried to keep count, but on a decent Saturday the girls would be pretty busy all through the night, with hardly any time at all to sit around and talk. There was also pretty good bar business on Saturday—less on Friday—and there was an average of two fights every Saturday night. One a little before midnight, usually, and the other between one-thirty and two. Geraldine told me at the beginning that that would be the pattern and it usually came out just about that way.

The fights were a pain in the neck but I got so I looked forward to them. I knew they were going to happen sooner or later and I wanted to get them over with. They were the same damned sort of fights the apple pickers used to have in upstate New York. Two guys who were lifelong buddies would try to beat the hell out of each other after a few drinks, and the next week they'd be buddies again.

I had a club to settle fights with but I hardly ever had to use it. See, with most of the guys, they would get drunk enough to start a fight, but not so drunk that they didn't know what they were doing. And one thing they were careful not to forget was that all they had to do was pull a knife or break something and Geraldine would bar them from the Lighthouse forever. Which meant they would be limited in terms of sex to their hands and their sheep and their sisters. They might chance getting killed in a fight, but they sure as hell didn't want to be barred.

So what I learned to do was sort of let it be their idea to take the fight outside. I'd walk through the room calling out, "Awright now, all you boys, let's clear the way for these two. They're trying to take it outside and you better stand back and make a path for them."

Now nine times out of ten there would already be a path for them big enough to drive a tank through, because as soon as one guy yanked a chair back everybody but the guy he was squaring off against would get the hell out of the way. But since the others would be backing off at the same time that I was doing my number, it sort of looked as though they were following my orders and opening a path to the doorway. And the fighters were left with the notion that *they* were the ones who wanted them to go outside and the crowd had been stopping them.

So out they went.

I never followed them outside. Others would, and would form a ring around them, and the watchers more or less made sure that nobody got too cute with a knife or kept on going after the fight was supposed to be over. There were two reasons why Geraldine didn't want me to do anything more than get them out. For one thing, she was afraid a whole crowd might turn on anybody who did too thorough a job of policing an outside fight. For another, she didn't really give a damn if they killed each other six ways and backwards, as long as they did it outside.

A couple of times I had to hit guys. My club was a steel bar with a thick wrapping of leather, and it scared the hell out of me. If I hit someone too hard I could easily kill him and if I hit too soft I could get a knife in my ribs. Since I am (a) basically non-violent and (b) a coward, I didn't want either of these things to happen. Sheriff Tyles had given me lessons on just how much force to use and said I had the touch down pat, but I figured there was a difference between the rifle range and the field of battle, and I wasn't all that confident I would do it right.

The first time was when a kid about my age knocked the neck off a beer bottle and started after another kid. I missed his head.

He got a broken collarbone out of the deal and I got an extra ten bucks from Geraldine.

Another time one guy pulled a knife and started moving in on his cousin, I think it was. I managed to come up behind him, which helped me keep my cool. I gave him the right kind of tap on the head and it worked just the way it was supposed to.

Now both of those times were exciting enough so that I would just as soon never have them happen again, but that still doesn't change the fact that they were rain on the desert.

I mean, nothing else really happened.

"I'm not really a bouncer," I told Geraldine once. "Not if you figure my occupation by the amount of time I spend on various chores. You know what I am?"

"What?"

"A hired chess player. And you ought to be able to hire somebody who could beat you once in a while."

"I like to win, Chip. And I don't suppose I could hire Sammy Reshevsky for five dollars a week."

"And room and board."

"You don't eat much. And the room is

there. I have four more rooms than I have a use for. Would you believe this was a seven-girl house when I opened it? There's not enough weekday trade now to support the two I've got. But if you just have one girl in a house it's a joke, and if a man has to have the same girl every single time he might as well marry her. I used to have seven and I used to collect twenty dollars on Saturdays. Now it's ten every day of the week. Everything costs more at every store in the county and what's the one thing that's dropped in price?"

"The Chamber of Commerce ought to advertise that. As a tourist attraction."

"Tourists? You wouldn't get tourists here if you gave it away. Bordentown. I never heard of anyone coming to Bordentown by choice."

I could have named one.

"Anyway," she said, "it's worth five dollars a week for a game of chess now and then."

So I played chess, and sent fights outside, and sat around a lot, and talked to Claureen and Rita, and ate eggs and grits and sausages for breakfast and hamburgers for supper, and around two or three or four in the morning Geraldine closed up and I went upstairs to

my room and got undressed and hopped into
bed and went to sleep.

Alone.

I suppose you find that hard to believe. So
do I, now that I think about it. I mean, you
may have gotten the idea by now that sex is
usually in the forefront of my mind, and if
you didn't get that idea you get a low score
in reading comprehension. Because it usually
is. In fact it just about always is.

But I never once had either Rita or Claureen,
and I never once had any of the weekend
girls. (I never really got to know the weekend
girls, as far as that goes; they were always
busy then, and so was I.) And obviously I
never had Geraldine. The tobacco farmer was
the only one who did all the time I was there.
I'm sure she could have given me the equiva-
lent of a college education, and I certainly
liked her as a person, but the only game I
ever thought of playing with her was chess.

But what stopped me with Claureen and
Rita?

Well, I wasn't interested.

It wasn't that they were unattractive. They
were pretty enough, but not in any meaning-
ful way. The best way I can think of to ex-

plain it is that you could sit and talk with them for an hour or so, and then when you left the room you would have a little trouble remembering what they looked like. I suppose that could be an advantage with a prostitute. I don't know.

But the thing is that the Mary Beth who wanted my bus ticket had turned me off prostitutes in general, and any of the fantasies I had toyed with about whores with various organs of gold just didn't hold up for me any more. And even if they had, for Pete's sake, I was sitting there every night while these girls went upstairs with men and then came back down and yawned and joked about it. I got to like them a lot in certain ways, especially Claureen. The two of them put together didn't have enough brains to make one reasonably intelligent girl, but I liked them. And they would have come to bed with me if I asked, either of them would have, and they more or less let me know this in a quiet way, but we all knew it would have made it awkward between us afterward. It wouldn't have been so awkward that I wouldn't have been willing to live with it if I had really wanted to ball them, but I didn't, so nothing ever happened.

Besides, after the first week or so I had my hands full with Lucille.

SEVEN

THE FIRST TIME I MET LUCILLE WAS THE first day I worked at her house. Minnie took me over that morning after Lucille had already left for school and introduced me to Rev. Lathrop, which was a little like being introduced to a tree or a mountain. I started in on chores and worked up to lunchtime, when Lucille came home to do the honors.

(One thing I'm evidently never going to get right is this business of calling meals by the right name. I grew up with the idea that what you had around noon was lunch, and what you had in the evening was dinner. In Bordentown they called it dinner at lunchtime and what they had at dinnertime was called supper or evening meal. I got this down pat while I was there but it's hard to keep it straight from a distance.)

Anyway, whatever you want to call it, Lucille came home from school and cooked something. And I introduced myself to her and she introduced herself to me (because her father was already too far gone to introduce us, assuming he remembered my name. Or her name, for that matter.) And I looked at Lucille, and Lucille looked at me, and all of a sudden there was enough electricity in the air to cause a power failure.

She was the cleanest, healthiest, prettiest little thing I ever saw in my life. She was really a shock after the East Village. See, for the past three months I had gotten used to girls who would live in a pair of dungarees and a surplus navy jacket. I'm not putting that down, because some of the girls I knew in New York were really beautiful, and with some of them you could sit and talk for hours at a time, really rapping on and on about everything. You could really relate to them as people, which is what it's all about and which makes everything much better.

But Lucille was something completely different. Short blonde hair all neatly cut and combed, and a short navy blue skirt and a powder blue sweater and blue knee socks and saddle shoes and a touch of lipstick on her mouth and a perfect complexion. One look at her and you knew that (*a*) she took two baths a day, seven days a week, and (*b*) she never got dirty in between, never even perspired.

When I think about it now, I can't stop thinking that there was nothing on earth a whole lot squarer than Lucille. Knee socks and saddle shoes, for Pete's sake. One look at her and you could hear Bill Haley and the Comets playing in the background. I mean, she looked like a cheerleader, which as it turned out she was, and in this day and age the idea of a girl hopping around like an idiot and doing the sis-boom-bah number for the basketball team is about as unhip as you can get.

Even the cleanliness thing, really, is overdoing it. Not that I'm in favor of being dirty, but there's a point where it gets ridiculous and you wind up with this feminine ideal of a girl who's been carefully wrapped in plastic wrap and never touched by the world. Girls are people, too, and it's more fun for every-body if you don't lose sight of this.

But I was really ready for Lucille, knee socks and saddle shoes and sis-boom-bah and all. It occurred to me that she looked pretty square, but it didn't occur to me that there was anything wrong with this. All I knew was that she looked good enough to eat, and it didn't matter much whether you called it lunch or dinner or coffee break.

Even so, it took me close to a week to do anything about it. It wasn't that she looked too pure to approach, because I could tell right away that she was reacting to me the same way I was reacting to her. But for awhile I had this feeling that if I so much as touched her hand I would be back in jail again, and this time it wouldn't be anywhere near as easy to get out again. I suppose this was partly because she was a minister's daughter and partly because I still felt like some sort of fugitive from justice. The trouble with getting by with a lie is that it's very hard not to go on worrying that the lie will catch up with you. I hadn't really done anything but change the truth a little in a few unimportant ways. Even so, it took me a while to be comfortable with myself. I felt, oh, as though I was on probation, I guess.

Another thing was that Lucille and I would spend an hour talking while her father was putting his food away in the back parlor. And the conversation was all things like how much trouble she was having with geometry, and how the basketball team was doing, and how her steady boyfriend was taking her to this dance, and how her friend Jeanie saw this really cool sweater in a department store in Charleston, and how Joan Crawford was her favorite actress, and things like that.

It's amazing the conversations didn't bore the hell out of me. I think if I had tapes of them I could use them to put myself asleep on bad nights.

I didn't get bored, though. I probably must have listened with only half of my head. One thing that helped, I think, was that she was younger than I was, and less experienced, and I wasn't used to this. The girls I knew were generally older and brighter and hipper than I was (which it isn't all that hard to be, actually).

I'm sure I would have gotten bored sooner

or later. But after about six days of this, with
our conversations never getting the least bit
personal or intimate and never even beginning to make the transition from talking to
rapping, I came up behind her while she was
carrying some dishes to the sink, and when
she turned around I lowered my mouth to
hers and kissed her.

The first time I took her bra off she made
so much noise I thought her father was going
to come upstairs. It was only the second time
we had gone upstairs. She had a small bedroom furnished largely in stuffed animals and
pictures of movie stars. The day before we
took her sweater off, and today we had her
bra off.

Her breasts were large, milk-white, creamy
pink at their tips. I don't know why in hell
she thought she had to wear a bra. I can't
really understand why any woman would har-
ness herself up that way, and Lucille was so
firmly built that she certainly didn't need
the support.

Of course I suppose a cheerleader without
a bra would really bounce all over the place,

but what's wrong with that? It would just increase the crowd at the basketball games.

"Oh, Chip," she said. "We shouldn't be up here."

I was too busy kissing her to answer her.

"You make me feel so funny. I never felt like this before. And you're so *fast!*"

There's a word you don't hear much anymore.

"'Cause I been dating Jimmie Butler for three years and steady dating him for two years in April and in all that time he never got as far with me as you did in a week. I'll let him take off my sweater and reach in under the bra but not take it off, that's as much as I'll let him do, and you went and skipped over that step completely, and how long have we known each other? Two weeks?"

The next day she made the old man's dinner in five minutes flat and went upstairs without being asked. I paid a few minutes' attention to her breasts and then put a hand under her skirt.

She pushed my hand away, snapped her legs together, sat bolt upright and crossed her arms over her breasts. She looked so frightened that at first I thought her old man had walked into the room or something.

She said, "Chip, I never should have let you kiss me. At first I thought you were never going to get around to trying, and then you did, and right then I should have known what was going to happen."

"Nothing happened, Lucille."

"What you just tried to do."

"I wanted to touch you. That's all."

"You wanted to touch me under my skirt."

"Uh-huh."

"Oh, my *God*!"

"Hey," I said. I put a hand on her bare shoulder and she jumped. "Hey, calm down," I said. "Take it easy."

"Jimmie Butler doesn't even *try* touching me there. He knows if he tries that I just won't let him touch me at all. We'll go out every Friday and Saturday and park in his car for hours and he never so much as tries to do that."

The past Saturday, Jimmie Butler had been a customer at the Lighthouse. He had three quick beers for courage and went upstairs and spent ten dollars with Jo Lee. That worked out to about five dollars a minute. "All the rabbits ain't out in the fields," Jo Lee said afterward.

"Because he knows I won't let him do anything if he tries to touch me there," Lucille was saying.

"Why?"

She looked at me, wide-eyed.

"Why won't you let him?"

"I won't let anybody."

"Why not?"

"Because I want to be *pure*, Chip."

I looked into those wide blue eyes, and then I closed my own, and when I opened them she was still there.

"I want to be pure on my wedding night," she said. "The way you look at me—"

I said, "What does a hand up your skirt have to do with being pure?"

"Chip!"

"Because it doesn't make sense to me, Lucille."

"One thing can lead to another."

"One thing's supposed to lead to another. That's what life is all about. Life is just one damn thing leading to another."

"Chip, nobody *ever* touched me there."

"How about you?"

"Me?"

"Don't you ever touch yourself there, Lucille?"

Her face had gotten gradually whiter during the course of the conversation. Now all the color that had drained out came back in a rush, until most of the blood in her body must have been in her head. She looked like a sunburn ad.

She hugged her breasts. There were tears in her eyes, and I felt awful.

"Hey," I said. "Easy, honey."

"Oh, Chip," she said, and buried her face in my chest. I put my arms around her and rocked her gently. She was sobbing her heart out.

"Easy," I said. "Baby, it's completely normal. Everybody does it."

"It's a sin."

"Lots of things are, if you believe everything they tell you. But the thing is that it feels good."

"I—"

"And makes a person more relaxed."

She drew back, looked at me with pain in her eyes. "I hardly ever used to do it," she said. "Just a little once in a while before I

122

went to bed, if I was feeling dreamy. And I would stop before anything happened. But these past few days—"

"Take it easy, honey."

"—I'm just so *terrible*! And I'm so ashamed of myself. I go back to school and I can't sit in my seat, and I go to the bathroom, and I, I, I, oh, *Chip*!"

"It makes you feel better, doesn't it?" She hesitated, then nodded miserably. "It feels good, doesn't it? And then it relaxes you."

Another nod.

"But you feel bad about it because you think it's a sin."

"Well, it is."

"Then everybody's a sinner," I said. And I told her that everybody did it except for people who were too stupid to figure out how, and that people scratched other parts of their bodies when they itched, and rubbed their muscles when they hurt, and what was the difference? By the time I was finished I sounded like a commercial for self-abuse, but she was sort of nodding along with me towards the end, and the panic scene was over.

So I just held onto her and kissed her a little in a friendly and nonsexual way, and then she remembered that it was time to go back to school, she would be late. She put her clothes back on and brushed her hair and lipsticked her mouth and went on her way, and I went downstairs and did the dinner dishes.

The next day I stayed above the waist and didn't say anything about yesterday's conversation. And out of the blue she said, "I did it again yesterday. Went to the bathroom and touched myself."

"So did I."

"You did?"

"Uh-huh."

"Do you always?"

"Sometimes."

(Actually that was the first time I had followed a session with Lucille with a session with myself. I had never really felt the need— our petting hadn't been all that frustrating, really. But after the conversation we had had and the little speech I gave her, it seemed to me it would be almost a matter of copping out if I didn't.)

"I never thought about that."

"I thought about you," I said. I petted her breast absently. "As a matter of fact, while

I was doing it I pictured you in my mind. Doing it."

"Oh, that's just *awful!*"

"Actually it was kind of nice." I propped myself up on an elbow and looked down at her. "You know," I said, "since we're both going to do it, why should we hide out in separate bathrooms? We could just do it here in your room before you go back to school."

She stared.

"It would be fun," I said. "We could watch each other."

"Chip, you are the most terrible boy I ever met."

I looked at her and her face went through some interesting changes. "Oh," she said, in a small, desperate voice, and I kissed her. She gave the kiss everything she had.

"I guess I'm terrible, too," she said.

"I'll tell you something that's even nicer, Lucille. Let me do it for you."

"Chip, don't talk that way."

"If you're going to do it anyway," I said reasonably, "it can't be any more of a sin if you use somebody else's hand. All you have to do is lie back and close your eyes and let your mind go anywhere it wants to. It's a lot better when someone else does it for you, you know."

"Is it?"

"And you feel a lot better afterward. You feel together inside instead of feeling all apart by yourself."

"That's how I felt yesterday. I felt tingly and I felt relaxed and I felt I was the only person in the world."

I lifted her skirt and put my hand on her thigh. She was so soft there.

"Chip, I'm afraid."

"Don't be."

"But I am, I am. Look how far we're going already and it's such a short time and, oh, you're not even my boy friend. Here I'm going steady with a boy I don't do half of this with, and I'm doing all this with you."

"It's what we both want, Lucille."

"I graduate high school a year from June. And after graduation I'll marry Jimmie Butler, and I want to be pure for him. I want to be a virgin, Chip."

"All I'll do is touch you."

"You promise?"

"Yes."

"I don't know if I can trust you."

"You can trust me, Lucille."

"Ohhh," she said.

I raised her skirt all the way and took off her panties. She didn't help and she didn't struggle either. Her face was so unhappy I almost felt like calling the whole thing off, but that would have been even worse for her.

I kissed her mouth, then her breasts, and I put my hand on her belly and let it move down to her. She was all soft and moist and warm.

She didn't get excited right away. I guess part of her was fighting it, but the other part of her won eventually and she panted and squirmed and made beautiful little sounds. She got almost there and hovered on the edge for a long time, trying to make it and trying not to make it, and I was starting to worry that it wouldn't work and she would wind up deciding that bathrooms were better than beds.

But then she got there, got all the way there, and in my mind I was there with her, feeling what she felt. I held her for a long time before I raised myself up and looked at her face.

She was glowing and she looked impossibly beautiful and I felt a lot like God.

EIGHT

THE FUNNY THING IS THAT I KEPT GET-
ting more and more involved with Lucille
without really getting involved with her at all.
We spent about fifty minutes out of every
lunch hour in her bedroom, but outside of
that we didn't see each other at all. I never
stayed around after she got home from
school, and on Saturdays she would generally
manage to spend the day with a girlfriend.
We never went to a movie or for a walk or
anything.

My job at the Lighthouse had something to
do with this. I was working during dating
hours, and the one night she could go out on
dates was the one night I really had things to

do there. But once I asked her if she'd like to catch a movie during the week and she said she couldn't.

"I have to stay with my father," she said. "You know that, Chip."

"He manages well enough Friday and Saturday nights, doesn't he?"

"Well, those are the only nights I can go out. I'm not allowed to date during the week."

"You could ask permission."

"Asking's not getting. Oh, Chip, I can't go out with you anyway. I'm going steady with Jimmie Butler, you know that, I told you a thousand times."

I said something about going steady being a Mickey Mouse institution.

She looked at me. "Do you think I ought to break off with Jimmie?"

"I guess not," I said.

That was the only time I ever asked her for a date, and I was just as glad she turned me down. I guess I wanted to keep this a lunchtime thing and not let it get very intense.

There were a couple of reasons for this. One of them makes me look like Mr. Nice Guy, so I'll throw it in first, and it was just that it wouldn't have been fair of me to take up all that much of Lucille's time. Because what Lucille wanted out of life was to get married as soon as she was done with high school and start having babies and spend the rest of her life there. And while that might not sound like something worth wanting, it was what she wanted, and it was probably what would be best for her. (Especially if Jimmie Butler developed a little control by doing the multiplication tables in his head or something.)

Anyway, Lucille wanted to be Mrs. Somebody. Maybe she would have been just as happy to be Mrs. Harrison as Mrs. Butler, but I really wasn't ready for that. She just wasn't that important to me, so I didn't want to become all that important to her.

The other reason was more selfish.

See, I was just having too much fun the way things were going. It was a fantastic ego trip for me, the whole thing, and even knowing something is an ego trip isn't enough to take the enjoyment out of it. For once in my life I was the teacher and she was the pupil, and I was getting a tremendous charge out of it. Instead of feeling like some utterly hopeless dope of a kid, I was the wise old man and she was the little innocent one. And every time I took her upstairs and let the stuffed animals watch me teach her something new and con her into doing it, well, it made me feel as if I was really somebody sensational.

(Which was another reason, I guess, that I had no desire to get in bed with Claureen or Rita. There was no way on earth I could feel like the wise old man with either of those two, and I guess I knew it would just bring me down in a bad way.)

By only seeing Lucille at lunch hour, I made that part of it be our entire relationship. And because we had so little time together we could just keep on going forward a little at a time instead of rushing straight into all-the-way sex. I didn't realize at the time that this was something I wanted. Instead I told myself it wasn't fair to rush her, that I wanted to let everything come at its own pace so it would be natural and good for her. But that was bullshit, really. Utter bullshit.

"You're like a drug to me, Chip," she said one day. "I just need more and more of you."

"Must be a good kind of drug. You look prettier every day."

"The girls ask me about you."

"What do they ask?"

"What you're like. Everybody knows about that place you work at. Some of them sort of want to go out with you. They want to come home with me and meet you. But they're scared of you at the same time."

"Scared of me?"

She nodded. "They think you must know things other boys don't. The things I could tell them! And sometimes I just could die for wanting to tell someone. I feel I could burst from holding it all inside me."

"I don't think it would be a very good idea to tell anybody."

"I know. I just say we hardly talk at all. That you don't even know I'm alive."

"Oh, I can tell you're alive, all right."

"Ohhhh—"

And a little later she said, "I'm scared of you, too, Chip."

"Oh, come on. You must know by now you can trust me."

"I know. But it used to be I could trust myself, and now I can t. I never knew I was like this."

"Aren't you glad you found out?"

"I don't know."

"Huh?"

"I just, oh, I don't know." Her face clouded, then suddenly brightened and she giggled. I asked her what was so funny.

"I was thinking about Jimmie."

"What about him?"

"If he could see us now."

If he could have seen us right then he would have come on the spot and saved himself ten dollars.

"He asked about you."

"What did you tell him?"

"Same as I told the girls. Not even that much. But I was thinking what would happen if I told him about you and me and all."

"He would probably kill one of us," I said. And if he had to choose, I thought, he would pick her. I had never mentioned to her that I had seen Jimmie now and than at the Lighthouse, so I couldn't tell her that he tended to back down pretty easily from fights. I didn't hold this against him, though. In fact I preferred him that way.

Her hand dropped onto me. "The other night," she said, "he wanted me to touch him."

134

"Did you?"

" 'Course not. I asked him what kind of a girl he thought I was."

"What did he say?"

"He apologized," she said, and giggled again. "He's just a baby, I guess. I never used to think so. Not until I met you."

Ego food.

At the beginning I thought I was going to get tired of her, maybe because she was so square. I suppose this would have happened if we had seen each other more, had dates and long conversations, or if I had met her friends or anything like that. But she left the boring part of her personality outside the bedroom, and once she stopped fighting the whole idea of sex she turned out to have quite a natural aptitude for it.

For a long time she spent half her time being passionate and the other half feeling guilty about it. At first she was very uptight every time we did something new, as if we were taking still another step along the road to Hell. This was fun in a way—first I taught her something new, and than I assured her it wasn't awful.

It wasn't long, though, before she wanted to do new things and came to bed looking forward to it. I guess what happened was that her mind finally realized I wasn't going to make her have regular intercourse, so she set that up in her mind as the one absolute sin and decided it was perfectly all right to do absolutely anything else.

So I taught her things I had done before, of which there were not too many, and things I had heard about or read about, of which there were a ton, and some things that I more or less invented. I'm not saying that I thought of things no one had thought of before because I'm not sure there are any of those things left, but they were new to me.

"My God," she would say. "When did you have time to learn all these things, Chip?"

She didn't know we were learning some of them together.

And she liked everything we did. Everything. I did oral things to her and taught her to do them to me, and she lived up to what Willie Em had told me about Southern girls.

And we tried anal things, which I hadn't done before. She didn't like the idea at the beginning, and she thought it would be painful and disgusting, and when we were done she said it was painful and disgusting and cried a little and I told her we wouldn't do it again.

And the next day she wanted to do it again and never said another word about it being painful or disgusting.

One day I brought a vibrator from the Lighthouse. I didn't tell Geraldine I was borrowing it. I didn't tell Lucille where it was from, either, but of course she would have had to know.

And finally one day we got our clothes off and got into bed and she asked me what I wanted to do, and I said we would just see what happened. And after a lot of things had happened she was lying on her back with her eyes closed and I was on top of her and our flesh touched.

She opened her eyes and asked me what I was doing.

I said, "I'm going to fuck you."

"All right," she said, and closed her eyes again.

Afterward she said, "I guess I should have let you do it right off. I knew it would happen the first day you kissed me. I knew it and I never forgot it and I was right, and we might just as well been doing it all along."

"Are you sorry?"

"Yes. No. I don't know."

"Did I hurt you?"

"Not enough to talk about. You hurt me worse other times and I never minded it. Will I get a baby now, Chip?"

"No."

"How come you're sure?"

I showed her the condom.

"It looks so silly," she said. "Did you buy it in a store or what?"

"I took it from—"

"From that place. I guess if Jimmie doesn't marry me I can always work there, can't I?"

"Don't talk like that."

"Knowing all you taught me. Unless you don't think I'm pretty enough."

"You're beautiful."

"I wonder do I look different now."

"No."

"I guess I'll call the school in a few minutes and say I can't come back today because my father needs me. I used to do that before you were working here."

"You don't have to worry, Lucille. No one can tell anything from looking at you."

"That's not why." She stretched and wriggled her toes. "I guess I don't want to get up and go putting on clothes again. I guess I liked what we did. I guess I want to do it again."

"Oh," I said.

"Do you have any more of those little things?"

"Uh, no."

"Can you use them more than once?"

"It's not a very good idea."

"Oh, well," she said. "There's other things we can do, I guess. An old boy named Chip taught me a whole roomful of them."

"You're an angel."

"I'm a devil is what I am. But I just don't care."

That was on a Friday afternoon in early March. I didn't see her at all over the weekend. I was hoping Jimmie Butler would come to the Lighthouse Saturday night and start a fight so that I could brain him with the club. Don't ask me why. Anyway, he didn't show up.

I almost went to church the next morning. Just a nutty impulse.

Monday morning I helped myself to a box of a dozen rubbers on my way out of the Lighthouse. We used one of them that lunch hour, and afterward she told me she almost broke up with Jimmie Saturday night.

"But I didn't. I wanted to, but I thought I'll wait until the proms are over and all, because he'd have to find somebody to take and everything, and it's easier to go along the way it is. And if I stopped going steady with him other boys might want to take me out, and at least I'm used to Jimmie. And I know I can handle him."

"Why did you want to break up?"

"Oh, I don't know. I just don't like being with him is all. And I hate it when he touches me. I just don't feel a thing. Sometimes I'll pretend I like it but I don't and it never does anything to me. He just keeps going with me now because it's a habit. He doesn't like it that I won't let him do any more than he used to do, but if he went out with anybody else he'd have to start all over at the beginning, so I guess he thinks I'm better than nothing."

"I think you're better than anything."

"I wouldn't marry him, anyway. Even if he wanted. I don't love him."

"Did you love him before?"

"No, but I didn't know it. I didn't know anything. Not knowing what I was missing, I guess."

I felt kind of weird. I had more than I had started out wanting in the first place, and I didn't know whether or not I wanted it now, or what I was going to do about it.

She said, "I love you, Chip."

I just wouldn't tell her that I loved her. She never asked for the words, not once, not even by throwing out hopeful pauses which you were supposed to fill with the words. And I just wouldn't say them.

I don't know why I made such a big deal out of it. I mean, *I love you* doesn't mean all that much. Nine times out of ten it's a polite way of saying *I want to ball you*, and you know it and the girl you say it to knows it and just saying the words doesn't send anyone out shopping for engagement rings.

The really dumb thing about it is that I could have said the words and meant them, because I *did* love her, whether or not I knew it at the time. I didn't want to spend the rest of my life with her, but that's not what the words mean anyway. I dug her and I cared about her and I enjoyed being with her and I wanted good things to happen to her and I, well, I loved her.

But instead of saying the words I even managed to keep them out of my own mind. I would ask myself things like, *Well, Chip kid, how will you get yourself out of this one? After all, old man, you've got to be gentle with the kid. You don't want to break her little heart.*

(I'll tell you something, I really hate writing all this down, because until just this minute I never realized what a complete asshole I was. I felt so goddamned adult with Lucille, and when I look back at it all now I can't believe I ever could have acted like such a shitty little snotnose. And I suppose a year from now I'll be apologizing to myself for being such an immature moron now.)

Of course I loved her, for Pete's sake. I loved her a lot more than she loved me, if you come right down to it, because I at least knew who she was and all, and what she knew about me was more lies than truth. She fell

142

in love with me, or thought she did, because I taught her what her body was for.

Maybe I loved her for about the same reason. Oh, the hell with it.

But figure this out. The day she told me she loved me, I sent a postcard to Hallie in Wisconsin.

NINE

SHERIFF TYLES SAID, "WELL, I HEAR TELL you got a salary increase, boy. I hear you're coming up in the world."

"Oh, I'm getting rich."

"Reckon Geraldine thinks a lot of you."

"It was because I finally won a game of chess," I said. "So she decided I ought to have an extra five dollars a week."

"You wouldn't be getting it if she didn't like the way you were doing the job."

"There's not much job to do. Playing chess with her is about three-quarters of the job." I took a sip of Coke. "Anyway, I don't guess it's enough to retire on."

He clucked. "Well, it's all in how you look

at it, isn't it? An extra five dollars a week, look at it that way and I'll admit that it ain't so much. But since you were only getting five dollars to start with, what you got amounts to a hundred percent increase, and I never heard of anybody kicking at a one hundred percent increase that they didn't even have to go and ask for. Even a goddamn nigger labor union ought to be happy about a hundred percent increase."

"I never thought of it that way."

He winked. "You keep doubling up that way, you'll be rich in no time."

"Guess you're right."

"On the subject," he said, "how you making out as far as money is concerned? You able to get by all right?"

"Oh, sure," I said. I had been buying clothes from time to time, and other things, and I was only making twenty a week from the two jobs—well, twenty-five now—but there was really nothing to spend money on. I even got my books free from the local public library, not because I was too cheap to buy a paperback but because the only ones in town were at the Atlantic station, and all they had were four shelves of swinging swapper garbage and one rack of Brian Garfield westerns. Every once in a while I would go back to see if they got something new, but they never did. I guess they were waiting until they sold the ones they had.

The library had a lot of good books. The only trouble was that they had all come out before the Second World War. This was okay as far as the fiction was concerned, I could get into old stuff well enough, but when I wanted to figure out how to fix the Lathrop television set I ran into a stone wall. There was nothing in the card catalog under *Television*.

"I've even been putting some money aside," I told him.

"Thought you might be. Probably got more than enough for the fare to Miami, I'd say."

"Oh," I said. "Well, probably."

"Be summer in a few months," he went on. "Florida weather's no attraction that time of year. Not that it's a bargain here. Myself, I don't mind the heat one way or the other. I'll sweat on a hot day, but I never minded sweating. Must do a man good. Otherwise you wouldn't do it, the way I see it."

I said something bright, like "Uh-huh."

146

"Heat bother you much?"

"Not usually."

"Didn't think so. A Yankee, your typical Yankee, the heat'll get him and he won't mind the cold. With folks down here it's the other way around. The way some of us were complaining about the first week in February, and it wasn't all that cold. Of course our heat isn't the kind you'll get in a big city, where the buildings hold it in. Makes somewhat of a difference."

I nodded.

"Minnie was saying you really made a good impression on the Reverend. She'll see him Sundays after the service and as like as not he'll have a good word for you."

"I hardly ever talk to him."

"Well, I wouldn't let on in front of Minnie, but I wouldn't be all that surprised if that's what the drunken old sonofabitch likes about you. Last thing he wanted was for those old hens to saddle him with a nursemaid. Imagine the kind of person they'd be apt to pick. Some Salvation Army jackass with a ramrod up his ass who'd either be watering the old sonofabitch's whiskey or praying all over the place. Just for the sake of somebody leaving

147

him alone, I don't suppose the Reverend would even mind if you was screwing his daughter six times a week and twice on Sundays."

I came within inches of cardiac arrest. But the Sheriff went sailing right on, and I'm sure to this day he just tried to pick the least likely example he could possibly think of. He gave me a bad moment, though.

"And Geraldine's happy with you, too. Happier than she lets on. She don't let on much, that one, but I got to know her pretty good over the years. Had a place here for the longest time. Set it up herself. There was this woman she was working for who was doing wrong by everyone—girls, customers, law enforcement people. Geraldine, she opened up on her own and got the right backing and the right girls working for her and sent the other old bitch clear out of the state. She knows what she's doing, that one."

"I can believe it."

"In her day, wasn't a better-looking woman in the county. You can believe that one, too."

"I do."

"Wasn't that bad myself, in those days. Before Minnie's cooking." And he patted his paunch and let his eyes drift off to examine old memories. *Before Minnie, too*, I thought, and wondered if Geraldine and the Sheriff still got it together once in a while for Auld Lang Syne. On holidays and birthdays, say. I sort of hoped they did.

"She thinks a lot of you," he was saying. "She thinks you're a good man to have around the place. Me, I think you make a damn fine Deputy Sheriff." He clucked again. "Well, I'm running off at the mouth again, and you better get on back if you want your supper. Just thought I'd give you a few things to think about."

A couple of days later Geraldine said, "Mate in four, starting with Knight to King Five. See it?"

I studied it for a long time, then nodded and started picking up the pieces.

"Interesting thing happened in the next county over," she said. "Used to be two regular gambling places there. About a year ago Ewell Rodgers had a second coronary, and you generally only get three of them, and he closed up and went and sat on his rocking chair. The other place was run by a man named Morgan from East Tennessee. He was getting all of Ewell's crowd, and success must have gone to his head. He rubbed some people the wrong way that he shouldn't have. He got raided and arrested, and while he was sitting in jail waiting for someone to put up bail money, his place somehow or other caught on fire, and the fire department just happened to take a wrong turn getting there. Not a stick left. Morgan took the insurance money and bought the fastest car he could find and drove all the way back to East Tennessee with the gas pedal on the floor."

She got up and went behind the bar and came back with a Coke for me and her bottle of banana liqueur. I couldn't remember her ever bringing the bottle to the table before. Usually she took her glass back each time and refilled it.

She said, "I used to have gambling in here, you know. I must have told you that."

"I think you mentioned it."

"Did very well with the gambling. Then there was an election and I was let know that there wouldn't be any trouble if the tables and slots and all went, so they went. By the time it was all right to replace them, it just wasn't worth it. Ewell and that Morgan were doing good business and everything was off around here, I was down from seven girls to two, and I couldn't be bothered. When Ewell retired I don't mind telling you it gave me ideas. There was that much business open, and I was sure to get a good portion of it. And then when Morgan's place went up in smoke—"

She picked up her glass, looked at it, and drank it down. This was as surprising as the time I heard her swear. She always took the stuff in little sips, and a drink would last her so long that I doubt she actually drank more than half of it; the rest evaporated.

"I would have six tables for cards," she said. "No more than that. Five tables of poker and one of blackjack. On the poker you let the deal pass and just charge so much an hour to sit in the game. No cutting the pot. Morgan was cutting pots there at the end.

"On the blackjack, you would have to have a dealer. I could deal it myself, as far as that goes. Any fool can. The only problem is if you have a dealer working for you and you can't trust him, because a blackjack dealer can think of fifteen different ways to cheat the house and you'll be forever trying to keep up with him."

She poured herself another drink. And drank it right down.

"And one craps table," she said. "That's all you would need. You let the players run the game, same as the poker. Then what I would do is slap slot machines all over the place. You make a ton on slot machines and all you have to do is take out the money and put a drop of Three-In-One Oil in the works once a month. No one ever lost money on a slot machine. Except the damned fools who play them."

"Where would you put all of this?"

"Right here in this room. It's big enough so there'd be space left over, no one would be crowded."

"What about the drinkers?"

She filled her glass but left it on the table. "Over on the right. Nobody ever goes in that room and you wouldn't know it's there, but it wouldn't be anything to put a bar in there."

"I don't know," I said. "You'd never fit our Saturday crowd in there unless you packed them like sardines."

"Chip, you wouldn't want that kind of

crowd if you had gambling. I don't even want them now, but there's not enough money just in the girls and I have to have every drink sale I can get. Put in tables and the idea would be to cut that crowd to a third of what it is. Maybe less than that, maybe a fifth, say, on Saturdays."

"Some of those drinkers wind up going upstairs."

"And most of them don't. Instead they make noise and start fights, and that's the last thing you can tolerate when you have gambling tables."

"How would you cut the drinking crowd?"

"Easiest thing in the world. Leave out the beer taps. Sell imported beer by the bottle at seventy or eighty cents. Push the hard liquor price up to a dollar a drink, nothing cheaper. The way it is now, we're selling girls to men who come here to drink. The other way, we'd be selling whiskey to men who come here for girls and gambling. And when a man's gambling he doesn't mind paying high prices for whiskey, and when he wins he likes to celebrate with a girl."

"You've got it all figured out," I said.

She drained her glass. "It's not something

that just came to me in a flash. I've been thinking about it."

"Without the drinking crowd, I guess you wouldn't have much need for a bouncer."

She didn't seem to hear me. "There won't be anybody opening up over the county line. And there won't be anybody else opening up here as long as Claude Tyles is Sheriff, and they won't get him out without burying him. Nobody even bothered running against Claude in the last election. He's well liked, Claude is. Not that he likes that many people himself. It's a rare person that Claude Tyles takes a shine to.

"Nobody else opening up, and all the gambling trade in this county and the next one. The drink business would go down but the profits would go up, and less aggravation involved. Be a five-girl house in no time at all, maybe go all the way up to seven girls if it worked that way. And with gambling, business spreads out more. It doesn't all concentrate on Saturday night. Might even raise the price on the girls to fifteen dollars. And they'd be making tips on top of that with the right kind of crowd."

She poured herself another drink. If it was affecting her, I couldn't see how.

"Make more money on drinks and more money on girls, and that's not counting what the gambling brings in. I haven't made that kind of money in so long I have trouble recollecting what it feels like."

She drank her drink.

"Only one thing wrong," she said.

"What's that?"

Her eyes locked with mine. "I'm too old to be bothered with it. It means all that work and concentration, and I ask myself what's the point? Would you like a drink instead of that Coke, Chip?"

"No, thanks."

"What I should be doing is cutting down, not building up. I'm not ready to pack it all in yet. Not this year. If I closed up now I'd die of boredom. But you feel yourself slowing down, you know. You feel yourself getting sick of people. The customers. You don't have the patience to put up with them. Little signs like that. Another couple of years, next year or the year after that, and it won't be a bad idea to get out of here and live in a big hotel in Puerto Rico and let people fetch me things.

I have money saved. Not enough to do it in style, but more than a little."

She gave her head a shake. "But if I expanded I'd have all I need and then some. Thing is, I'd have things just about ideal by the time I wanted to retire. And who in the world would take it over? Rita and Claureen between them couldn't run a pool hall. They couldn't run a race. Two days of operating this place and the whole thing would fall apart.

"In fact, they couldn't even help me out enough in getting things organized. I'd need a man, and he would have to be somebody smart and sure of himself, somebody who could get on good with Claude Tyles, somebody who wouldn't rub the girls the wrong way or be after them all the time. And assuming I had the luck to turn up someone like that in this part of the country, which is as likely as mucking out a stable and finding an emerald, why, what chance in the world would there be that he'd be someone I can trust?"

"I see what you mean," I said.

Her eyes challenged me. "Do you?"

"Well, uh, sure."

"I wonder if you do. You think about it, Chip. You think about it, and one of these days I'll bring up the subject and then we'll talk about it some more. Meanwhile you just give my problem some thought, will you?"

The thing is, subtlety generally sails right on past me. When Geraldine first started opening up that night I wondered why she was telling me all this, and I decided she just wanted somebody to use for a sounding board, bouncing words off me when she was actually talking to herself. And I figured she picked me for the same reason that she played chess with me—I was working for her, and I didn't have anything better to do.

She closed for the night as soon as we finished talking, and I went upstairs and got undressed for bed. And I stretched out and put my head on the pillow and closed my eyes, and then I immediately opened them and sat up and switched the light on.

She hadn't just been talking *to* me. She had been talking *about* me.

(Of course when you read this it's probably pretty obvious all along, especially because I put her conversation right after the one with

157

the Sheriff. But that other conversation wasn't even in my mind when I sat listening to Geraldine, so maybe it should have been obvious to me anyway, but not as obvious as it seems.)

Anyway, I sat up in bed and figured out what it was all about. Sheriff Tyles thought I should stay in Bordentown, and said that Geraldine thought the world of me. And Geraldine wanted to expand the business but couldn't do it without the help of some man who was capable and honest and had an in with the Sheriff, someone she liked and trusted, someone who could take over the whole operation when she was ready for complete retirement.

Which meant that I had found the one thing I never even thought to look for in Bordentown.

A Job With A Future.

I got up and walked around the room a little. I had that sensation in my mind and body of having had too much coffee and all I had was one cup with supper. I just kept pacing, and then I went down the hall to the bathroom only to find out that I didn't really have to go after all. Just nerves, I told myself nervously, and went back to my room and paced the floor again.

A Job With A Future. A Position With Real Opportunities For Advancement.

I couldn't believe it.

Because, after all, that was the one thing I had been looking for ever since they booted me out of Upper Valley Preparatory Academy. I left that stupid school determined to make my way in the world and do all the good old Horatio Alger type things and work my way up in the world. And I never got anywhere. In fact I never got close to getting anywhere, because I kept getting idiotic jobs and drifting into idiotic situations.

Until finally the most idiotic situation of all brought me to Bordentown, a town that barely offered opportunities for stagnation, let alone advancement. And instead of one idiotic job I got two of them, and instead of trying to make my mark in the world I just tried to stay alive and let time pass, figuring that sooner or later I would get up and get out of Bordentown, but not even being in any rush to do that because the whole idea of getting ahead in the world seemed like something I was never going to get around to.

(If you really knock yourself out trying not to end sentences with prepositions, that last sentence would wind up *seemed like something around to which I was never going to get.* I mean, it's an awkward sentence anyway, just sprawling all over the place, but I think it would be even worse if it didn't end with a preposition. Or two prepositions, actually.)

Some of the kids I knew in New York were very much into Zen, and one girl made me read a description of Zen Archery, in which you don't exactly aim the arrow at the target and don't exactly ever let go of it. You just become part of the bow and arrow and let yourself happen along with the bow and the arrow, and somewhere along the line the arrow goes from your fingertips to the target. It read very nicely, but I wasn't sure if it made any sense. The girl said it was easier to understand if you were stoned. I tried to get stoned a couple of times but nothing happened. Now, though, I was beginning to understand.

Because this seemed to me like a case of Zen Advancement, of Zen Making-One's-Way-In-The-World. I hadn't tried to do anything, just sort of becoming part of Borden-

160

town and letting the rest happen, not even pointing myself at the target, not even letting go of the string.

Bull's-eye!

TEN

"YOU SEEM DIFFERENT," LUCILLE SAID.

"I do?"

"Maybe not," she said. She yawned and stretched. She was lying on her back with one arm at her side and her other hand tucked palm-up under her head. I touched her armpit. (It's a shame there isn't a better word for it. When you hear the word *armpit* you think of deodorant. When I touched Lucille's, all secretly smooth and hairless, I didn't think of deodorant. I thought of other warm private places, and of better things to do with an armpit than rub deodorant on it.) I touched hers now, rubbing a little with the tip of my finger.

"Maybe it's me," she said.

162

"Maybe what is?"

"I don't know."

It was the middle of the week and the lunch hour was only twenty minutes over with. We had another half hour to ourselves and had already done what we did during lunch hours. Usually we would take our time, but this afternoon she didn't want to pause along the way and admire the view. She just wanted to get there full speed ahead, and she did and I did, and it was very nice.

But now she was in a mood, and it was something I wasn't used to with her. I asked her what was the matter.

"Oh, nothing," she said. "Just that you seem all wrapped up in thoughts lately, and you might as well be a hundred miles away."

"I'm right here," I said, and touched her to prove it.

She moved my hand away. "Have you been thinking things, Chip?"

"Nothing in particular."

"Oh."

"I always think things," I said. "I mean, I'm alone a lot, so I'll let my mind just wander off on its own some of the time."

"You like doing that?"

"It beats talking to yourself."

"I do that sometimes. Talk to myself. I don't think much, though."

"Uh."

"I guess you must think I'm awful simple."

"What makes you say that, Lucille?"

"I don't know. Maybe on account of it's true."

"I don't think so."

"Just an old preacher's daughter. Never been anywhere and never done anything."

"You've done a few things."

She sat up suddenly and put her legs over the side of the bed. Without looking at me she said, "Do you know what it's like when you start thinking things and you can't stop? You don't want to think them but there they all are in your head and you can't make them stop?"

"I know."

"Does it sometimes happen to you?"

"A lot of the time."

"It never happened to me before. I would just, oh, you know, I would just go along. Hardly thinking about anything, and if I ever had a thought that bothered me I would just whisk it off out of my head and not think about it anymore. Like a program on the television that you don't want to watch so you turn it off. But now I can't do that."

"What's bothering you?"

"You know what it's like? Like having that bad television program going on in a set that's inside of your head, and there's no way you can turn it off or pull the plug or change the channel, so what do you do?"

"Pray for a commercial," I suggested.

"Oh, you don't see what I mean."

"Yes, I do. I'm sorry, Lucille. It was just a dumb joke."

"No commercials and the program's never through, it just goes on. I reckon that's why Daddy drinks. You know he told me about it once. He said one day he looked into his soul and saw something there that he couldn't bear the sight of, and drink kept him from seeing it. And I always thought, well, why didn't he think on something else. I knew what he was saying but I thought if something like that ever happened to me I would just make the thought go away, but you can't, can you?"

"You want to talk about it, Lucille?"

"I guess not."

I put my arms around her and turned her face toward me. There were tears in the corners of her eyes.

I said, "Hey."

"Lemme be, Chip."

"If something's bothering you—"

"Oh, I'm making something out of nothing is all. Never had a thought in my head before and I'm just not used to it. Just a mood I'm in that I'll get over."

"Maybe it's your period coming on."

"You think so?"

"I don't know."

"Maybe that's what it is," she said.

What it probably was, I felt, was that she had gotten a contact high from my own moods. Because I couldn't stop thinking about what Geraldine and I had not quite discussed and what Sheriff Tyles and I had not quite talked over. Which was that I would stay in Bordentown and share the management of the Lighthouse with Geraldine, and together we would expand the operation and hire more girls and put in gambling tables, and in a year or two when she was ready to spend the rest of her days sipping banana liqueur in Puerto Rico, the Lighthouse would be mine.

And I could see it all happening just that way.

I got a paper and pencil and did a little rough figuring, and then I threw the paper away because the numbers I was using were just ones I was picking out of the blue. And the numbers didn't matter, anyway, because you didn't need them to realize that the Lighthouse, run the way Geraldine was talking about running it, couldn't help but make a fortune.

I mean, it wasn't just a matter of being secure and established and successful.

I'd get rich.

It wouldn't be hard, either. At first I thought that Geraldine only thought I was right for it for the same reason that she thought I was fit to play chess with. There just weren't that many people around to choose from. But I had to admit it went further than that. I *was* honest, and I *did* get along well with the girls, and I seemed to have a feeling for handling the customers, and Sheriff Tyles, who she said didn't take to many people, had done everything on earth short of adopting me. On top of all that, I kind of liked the business itself. I had always thought that the only reason anyone would want to go and live in a whorehouse was so he could have his pick of the whores, but I hadn't picked one of them yet and I really liked living there. I mean, I felt at home there.

And as far as the gambling part of it was concerned, I suppose I was suited for that, too. I had played cards a few times without getting caught up in it, and I couldn't imagine ever risking anything important on whether two pair was the best hand at the table or what number would come up on the next roll of dice. And why anyone would drop a perfectly good quarter in a slot machine was beyond me.

Now it seems to me that the one thing you wouldn't want to be if you ran a gambling operation is a gambler. It was like a blackout alcoholic owning a liquor store, or a sex maniac running a whorehouse. You would just eat up all the profits. And at the time I was kind of interested in gambling in a spectator-type way. I mean, as long as it's not my money, the excitement's fine.

I would be rich, and I would be comfortable with what I was doing, and I would be good at it. The whole thing would be officially illegal, but there are laws and laws. And even if Sheriff Tyles stopped being sheriff sooner or later, by then I would be one of the important men in Bordentown. It doesn't take all that much to be one of the important men in Bordentown, it's not like being President of the United States. I would be important.

I kept just playing all of this through my mind. It was like Lucille had said, a television set in your head that you can't turn off.

The thing was, I liked the program.

Of course thinking about all this made me think about Lucille, too, because she was part of it. Until I talked with Geraldine (or listened to her, because she was the one who did all the talking) I took it for granted that I was going to leave Bordentown sooner or later. I was in no rush, and I had more or less forgotten all that business about Miami, until the Sheriff reminded me, but I would be leaving sooner or later.

And, although I didn't like to dwell on it, when I left Bordentown I would also be leaving Lucille.

Oh, once in a while I would play around with the thought of taking her with me. But I don't think I ever gave that any serious consideration. In Bordentown, for an hour a day five days a week, she was perfect. In the rest of the world, and on a full-time basis, she just wouldn't work out. (Maybe that line makes me sound like a shit, but it's honest. She wouldn't work out for me and I wouldn't work out for her and it's silly to pretend otherwise.)

But if I stayed in Bordentown, that meant I would eventually marry Lucille.

In that kind of situation, she would be perfect, actually. It was her home town and she belonged there. The idea of the preacher's daughter marrying the keeper of the cathouse sounds pretty ridiculous, but I can't think of anybody who would have gotten really uptight about it. Except maybe her father, but who was going to tell him? And why should he pay attention?

It would be perfect for Lucille, and in that situation she would be the perfect wife for me. And what I always wanted was a job with a future and a girl who loved to have me make love to her. Which meant I would be getting everything I always wanted.

That was the whole trouble.

* * *

I once read a book by Fredric Brown called *The Screaming Mimi*. (I also read about twenty other books by Fredric Brown, and there wasn't one I didn't like. I like lots of books, but I don't always finish one feeling that I'd really like to meet the author sometime. I always feel that way about Fredric Brown.)

Anyway, this book starts with two drunks sitting on a bench, and one of them says that you can always have what you want as long as you want it badly enough. (The catch is that, when you don't get it, that just goes to show that you didn't want it badly enough.) The other guy sees a beautiful girl pass by and says that what *he* really wants is to spend a night with her, and for her to be stark naked.

Well, this happens at the end, only it isn't quite the way he hoped. (I don't want to spoil the book for you.) But the ultimate point, the philosophical point, is that if you want something badly enough you *will* get it, sooner or later, and then you'll find out that you don't want it anymore, and maybe you never really wanted it in the first place.

So this is what kept going through my mind, not steadily but off and on. It was all there, and all I had to do was reach out and take it.

But did I still want it?

I liked Bordentown, but I wasn't sure I wanted to live there permanently. I mean, I like swimming, but I'd hate to spend the next fifty years in the middle of the ocean. And more important, there was this major question of identity that was suddenly bothering me. I liked the idea of running the Lighthouse and putting down roots there and all, but I wasn't convinced that it was me.

Oh, even the way I was talking, the South Carolina accent. I wasn't consciously putting it on. I talked that way without thinking because everybody else talked that way and I tend to fall into the patterns of wherever I am. But if you woke me up in the middle of the night I wouldn't sound that way. So it felt natural when I did it but it really wasn't, not inside.

And the attitudes I had. Like being against long-haired hippies and black people and Yankees and everything else. It didn't particularly bother me to act that way, or to use the word *nigger*, for example, because as far as I was concerned it was just part of doing the

Bordentown thing for as long as I happened to be there.

But if I was there forever I would be doing all of that business forever, and when you do something long enough either it becomes real for you, which might be bad, or else you spend your whole life living a lie, which might be worse.

If I stayed in Bordentown, it meant I would probably never in my life rap with anybody the way I had rapped with some friends in the East Village, the way I rapped with Hallie the one night I spent with her. I might make a lot of friends, and I might get to know them very well, but they would never really get to know me.

Even Lucille. I could marry her and live with her for the rest of my life, and she would never really know who I was. Even if I didn't try to keep anything from her, even if I opened up completely. There was no way for me to get through to her that completely.

And sooner or later that part of me that no one knew about wouldn't even be there any more. Because I would be the only one who knew about it, and I would tend to forget.

This scared the hell out of me.

*   *   *

The trouble with writing all this down is that there's no real way to get across exactly how I felt from day to day. See, it was never a constant thing. It was a seesaw, really. I would feel very strongly one way on one day, and the next day I would feel very strongly the other way. And after a little while of this I would be aware of the pattern myself, I would know while I was feeling like staying in Bordentown that the next day I would feel like running for my life. When you get like that it's really terrible because you're afraid to trust yourself. You don't dare make a decision because you know that whatever you decide will seem like the wrong choice in a day or two.

If I left, that was the end of it. I could never come back, and I would probably never have a chance like this for the rest of my life. And if I stayed I would gradually get in deeper and deeper, and we would expand the Lighthouse, and I would marry Lucille, and by the time I realized I should have left, I would be too tied down and it would be too late, and I would spend the rest of my life regretting that I didn't get out while I had the chance.

What I wanted to do was keep my options open as long as possible, but you can't, really, not for very long.

Lucille helped keep me sane, or as close to sane as I was. My moods kept switching and she was vaguely aware of this but she had her own moods to contend with. And no matter what mood either of us was in, those lunch hours in her bedroom helped. I always wanted to make love to her, and she always wanted me to, and it always worked. Sex isn't the only thing in the world, despite what you might read in *The Swinging Swappers*. But when it's good it can do a lot to take your mind off the other things.

Until finally one afternoon I got so groovily lost in her warm body, so completely out of myself and away from myself, that when the world settled together again all I could think of was how much I owed her. Not what I felt for her, or what future I wanted with her or without her, but how much I owed her.

I wanted to give her something, and it seemed to me that I wasn't giving her enough. I wasn't even sharing thoughts with her, and I couldn't do that, not yet, but there was one thing I could give her, one phrase I had been holding back all along for no good reason at all. There were words I could say that she had been waiting to hear, and I could say them whether they were true or not.

I turned and looked into her eyes, and she looked back into mine. And I said the three words she had been waiting so long to hear:

"I love you."

And she looked back at me, drinking the words, her eyes widening as she heard them. And she opened her mouth hesitantly, and I heard the echo of my own words in my head and waited for her to speak.

And she said three words back to me:

ELEVEN

"CHIP, I'M PREGNANT."

TWELVE

"GERALDINE? THERE WAS THIS THING I was sort of wondering about."

"What we talked about awhile ago? I thought you might have been thinking about it."

"Well, I was sort of doing some heavy thinking about the business. And then this one little point got stuck in my head, and I thought I would just ask."

"Be my guest."

"Well, I was sort of wondering what you would do if one of the girls, if Rita or Claureen, if one of them got pregnant."

"I'd be powerfully surprised," she said. "Rita's step-aunt did a knitting needle abortion on her when she was fourteen, and they had to take out some of the parts you need if you want to have a baby. And Claureen had to go to the hospital for a scraping a year and a half ago and while he was in there the doc tied off her tubes."

"Well, Jo Lee or Marguerite, then. I mean, you know, any girl who happened to work here."

"Just any girl."

"That's right."

"Any girl at all."

"Uh-huh."

"Like Lucille Lathrop, even."

"—"

"Chip, I'm an old woman. I've been years in the same business and seen every kind of man there is to see, and I can tell whether a man's getting it or not, or if he's the kind of man who wants it or not. And I know you're getting it, and getting it regular, and I know you like what you're getting. And you're not getting it here where it's all over the place for the taking, and you're not out catting around, so where else *would* you be getting it?"

"You've known all along?"

"Took it for granted."

"Does anyone else—"

"Claude Tyles asked what you were doing for love, and I imagine I led him to think you were alternating between Rita and Claureen. When did you find out she was pregnant?"

"This afternoon."

"How long gone is she?"

"Almost two months."

"She's sure about it?"

"She seems to be."

"Instead of stealing rubbers from around here, you should have told me and I would have gotten pills for her. You can't count on rubbers, don't you know that? Well, that's under the bridge. What do you want to do?"

"I don't know."

"Marry the girl? Have an abortion? What?"

"I don't know."

She did something odd. She put her hand on top of mine for a minute, then gave a squeeze and took her own hand back.

She said, "Chip, if she just told you today then you're in a bad way. You sure she didn't tell you a week ago?"

"No. Why?"

"You didn't suspect until today?"

"Never."

"Because you've been walking round in grand confusion for better than a week, and if it's not that it's something else, and now with this on top of it you must be in a bad way."

"I guess I am."

"Chip, I'm too old to get shocked or disappointed or anything but older, and I can't even get that too much. I'm not much for questions. But you got something that you got to tell to somebody, and I guess I can do a better job of listening than most. You can just put it straight out and not stop first to think how it'll sound."

I didn't say anything.

"Or you can tell me to forget it and I will. I'm good at forgetting. I can forget just about anything."

"No," I said. "I was just trying to figure out where to start."

The words were all there waiting, and once I opened the valve they poured out. A couple of times she filled in with a question but she didn't have to do that very often. I just went ahead and talked until there were no words left. I probably said the same thing half a dozen times in different ways. If I repeated myself, she pretended not to notice. She sat there and took it all in until I was done.

Then she went to the bar and came back with a water glass full of something. She handed it to me and I looked at it.

"Just plain corn," she said. For a minute I thought she was referring to what I had said. "Corn whiskey," she said. "Drink it."

"The whole thing? It'll kill me."

"The state you're in, it would take a quart before you'd feel a thing. All this'll do is settle you some. Go ahead and drink it."

I finished it in three gulps. It went down like fire. I guess it settled me some.

"Now I'll tell you a story, Chip. Story about a girl like Rita or Claureen, just a down-home girl who wasn't much and wound up going with men for money. Her pa ran off when she wasn't more than a bit of a girl and all she ever had from him was a postcard once in a while. Maybe she built him up a little in her mind but not all that much. Then one day after she's been hustling for a time she hears from one of her aunts that got a telegram from Norfolk. My . . . this girl's father was in a fight in a waterfront bar and some sailor broke a bottle over his head and he's in the hospital with his skull fractured.

"So this girl goes to Norfolk to see her pa, and he's in a hospital there. She visits him but he's in a coma, and after a week he dies without ever coming out of it. And she makes arrangements to ship the body back here to be buried next to my mother.

"Now while this girl was in Norfolk . . . that's two slips so far, I suspect you could put a name to this girl if you were pressed, couldn't you? Doesn't matter. This girl, while she's in Norfolk, she meets this man and one thing leads to another. This man is in naval stores in Baltimore. A good family. He wants her to marry him and come on back to Baltimore.

"And it's like a dream to her. This man, he's rich, and he's a good man, and he wants her to marry him. But she thinks, Now, how can I marry up with him when I've got all this in my past? And what if he finds out?

"So she decides to tell him, and she tells him. And he says what does he care, because that's something that happened in South Carolina and what does it have to do with Baltimore, and as far as he's concerned it never happened at all, and it doesn't bother him one bit, and if it bothers her then she's a fool, and he knows she's not a fool.

"And she thinks, well, it'll bother him in the years to come. But if it ever does she never knows about it, he never once throws it back to her, as it turns out.

"So she goes to Baltimore, and they're married, and there were all these things she was afraid of, how his family would take to her and what his friends would think, and none of the things she worries about ever come to pass. She thinks maybe she'll meet someone from her past and it'll ruin everything, but none of this ever happens. There are all of these things she worries about and it turns out she needn't have worried about any of them, because none of them ever come to pass.

"And she's an intelligent girl, Chip. She has a good mind. She always educated herself and paid some mind to how people talked, and she goes on doing this in Baltimore, and his family and friends like her. They accept her completely. Completely. They never even think he married beneath him because they get to thinking that she comes from quality people down in South Carolina.

"She's there for three years, and in that space of time she sees that the things that worried her are nothing at all. And she has a child. A little boy."

She stopped talking and her eyes were focused into the distance at a point somewhere over my shoulder. Whatever she was looking at was in some other room.

"And one day she said *I'm not me no more.* And she put a few weeks into thinking on that, and one morning she left the baby with the maid and took a taxi downtown to the railroad station. She wouldn't look out that train window for fear she might get off at the next stop. She just sat there, this fine lady in these expensive clothes, and she stared straight ahead and didn't see a thing.

"She never looked back, ever.

"Whether they looked for her or not she never knew. She left him a note saying she was running off with another man. She figured if you want to hurt somebody you do it quick and clean, and if you want to do one thing decent it's to have the guts to make people hate you if it'll be easier for them that way. Because the hate won't reach you because you'll be out of it, and if it'll sear another person's wounds . . ."

She was silent for a long time, but I didn't say anything because I knew she hadn't finished.

Then she said, "Of course, she wasn't the same girl who went off to Norfolk three years earlier. She saw things in a way she never would have seen them before. She knew how to talk like a lady. She knew manners. But she could let them slide off and nobody knew the difference. Except for what she knew of herself.

"She was lonely, but she would have been that anywhere. She was where she deep-down belonged, whether it was better or worse for her to belong there. She never regretted it. She would be sad sometimes, and she would wonder what happened to that man in Baltimore, and to that baby. . . ."

In another voice she said, "Somewhere along the way it gets determined just what a person is, and for the rest of his life he's stuck with it. Whoever else he may try to be is just play-acting. I guess you know you'll have to go, Chip."

"I know."

"I guess you knew it all along."

"I guess I did."

"Once you got to do something, there's nothing but to do it. Tonight is better than tomorrow. You'll take my car."

"I can't—"

"It's no use to me. I haven't driven it myself in ten years. It's almost as old as you are. I don't guess it has as many miles on it, though. You can drive, can't you?"

"I have a license. I've used the Reverend's car a couple of times on errands."

"This has a stick shift. You know how to work it?"

"In a sort of academic way."

"You'll get the hang of it. I'll make the registration over to you. Oh, now, it's not so much. A 1954 Cadillac, what would I get selling it? Not even an antique yet. That star of yours will guarantee against a ticket anywhere in the state, and by then you'll be comfortable driving it. I let the girls use it. It runs all right. It's still a Cadillac. Always will be, old as it gets."

I said, "Lucille."

"You want to take her along?"

"I don't know."

"She would go."

"I know. I keep feeling I ought to take her."

"You could take her with you. But she'd never really *be* with you. No more than you could stay here. Listen to me. You can hurt her now quickly or spend fifty years killing her by halves. Because whether you stay here or take her with you one thing is sure, and that's that she will never complete you. And you would never tell her that but she would always know, and never know why."

I swallowed.

"The Sheriff will get a report and he'll tell her about it. You had an accident on a road out of town. You were driving my car, and you were in a wreck and were killed, and the body was shipped north for burial with your parents."

"The Sheriff—"

"Claude will tell her that. He'll get that report."

"How?"

"From me."

"Oh."

"Claude Tyles knows all a man has to know about who you have to be whether you want to or not. Sometimes what you have to do is stay. Not in a place, necessarily, but with a person. He had to, and he did, and he knows. For my part, I'll see she gets the baby taken care of. Whichever she wants, having it and then getting shut of it or just getting shut of it. If she's even pregnant in the first place, which we're none of us sure of. Chip?"

"What?"

"You can feel as guilty as you want to, but all it is is foolishness. What the two of you had was good for the two of you. Nobody can ask more than that. It's no kindness to take something good and keep it going when it's no good no more. She had a beautiful young romance and her lover died. Why, you'll be more in her memory than you ever could have been in her life."

She gave me a couple old suitcases of hers. I packed everything and put the suitcases in the trunk. I went back to say goodbye to her and she looked as though she wished I hadn't.

"You send me a card from time to time. Just so I'll have an idea of where you're at.

No need to sign it or the snoops at the Post Office'll have something to talk about. I don't get that much mail," she said. "I guess I'll know who it's from."

THIRTEEN

THERE WAS A STRETCH OF TIME THEN
when nothing happened you would want to
read about. I didn't do much but drive, and
I didn't work too hard at that, either. I would
push the old Cadillac until I came to a town
that looked decent enough and pick out one
of the large Victorian houses with a sign in
front that said TOURISTS or ROOMS or something of the sort. They would generally be run
by a widow living alone, or two old maids,
or a widow and her old maid sister, and the
rooms were clean and comfortable and only
cost two or three dollars a night, which was
less than half what the cheapest motel would
charge. Sometimes they included breakfast, or

LAWRENCE BLOCK

sold it to you for something ridiculous like fifty cents.

I stayed in so many of those places I have trouble remembering which was which. They were all the same in so many ways. There would always be a small portable television set, and it would be the only piece of furniture in the house that was less than thirty years old. There was usually a spinet piano in the parlor that no one had played in almost that long, and if I stayed more than a night the woman would ask wistfully if I played the piano, and would be sad to hear that I didn't.

"No one ever does," she would say. "I suppose I ought to sell it for all the use it is, but I cannot bear to, Mr. Harrison. I just cannot bear to sell that piano."

If they all sell them all at once, the market for second-hand pianos is going to collapse overnight.

There were always framed photographs on the piano, and on the carved sideboard in the hallway. You could tell the frames were silver because they were usually slightly tarnished. And there was generally a vase of cut flowers on the sideboard next to the photographs, and there were potted plants all over the place. The plants were usually green and healthy.

Sometimes there would be a cat or a dog. More cats than dogs, all in all. The cats tended to keep to themselves. The dogs tended to be very small, and bark a lot, primarily at me.

I couldn't tell you just how many houses like this I stayed in, or how much time I spent this way. I wasn't very much involved in time, for some reason. I would be very conscious of the time of day because as soon as it was nine or ten at night I could go to bed and not think about anything until it was time to get up the next morning. But I didn't bother with days of the week, or what month it was, or that sort of thing. I didn't read newspapers or look at television. I knew there was a whole world out there but I didn't want to think about it. I had a bath every night and put on clean clothes every morning and when my clean clothes began to run short I did a load of wash in my current landlady's washing machine. Some of them didn't have washing machines of their own but knew a neighbor who would let me use theirs.

Sometimes I stayed one night and then left, particularly if there was a yipping dog in the house, or if there were other boarders. If I felt like staying, I would have a look around the house for something that needed fixing. Usually I didn't have to look very hard because the woman would apologize for whatever it is.

"You'll have to forgive the appearance of that room because it needs repapering, Mr. Harrison" . . . "The boy who used to do my yard work was drafted into the Army last month, Mr. Harrison, and I just can't keep up with my rose beds" . . . "I don't know how this house can go another year without painting, Mr. Harrison, but I had a man out to give me an estimate and, land, the price he asked!"

I changed a lot of faucet washers and replaced a lot of broken panes of glass. I cleaned out some basements and mowed and reseeded lawns and trimmed shrubbery and hauled trash. I patched plaster, which wasn't as hard as I thought it would be, and I put up wallpaper, which was. In Columbia, Missouri, I painted a whole house without falling off the ladder once. I guess that summer of apple-picking was valuable.

That was for the woman who hadn't known how the house could go another year without painting. She told me this at breakfast, and it was a breakfast that came free with my three-dollar room rent, and it was such a good breakfast and such a clean comfortable house that I figured I wouldn't mind spending another week or two there.

So I said, "Well, I could paint it for you."

"But I couldn't afford it. The size of this house, and he wanted nine hundred dollars."

"If you'll pay for the paint and brushes, and find out where I can borrow a ladder, I'll do it for five dollars a day and my keep."

"Why, I just can't believe that, Mr. Harrison! How can you afford to do that?"

"Well," I said, "I don't have all that much else to do, actually."

It was really very satisfying doing things like that. With that house, I saw that she bought the best paint, and I took my time and did a good job. At the beginning I'm sure she was scared to death I would fall off the ladder and kill myself. The same thing had occurred to me. But I didn't, and the house got painted, and I slept ten hours a night in my room and ate three good meals a day, and when I washed out my brush for the last time she paid me fifty dollars and couldn't believe that was all it was going to cost her.

"It looks so fine now," she said, walking around the house and admiring it from every angle. "It hasn't looked so fine since he was alive. You don't know what it's been like, Mr. Harrison, thinking I would never live to see it looking right again."

It made me feel good to leave a place in better shape than I found it. Sometimes I felt like Johnny Appleseed and other times like the Lone Ranger.

And I needed that kind of feeling, because if I let myself think about other things, about Bordentown things, I didn't feel like Johnny or Lone. I just felt like a son of a bitch.

That first night, driving the Cadillac generally north and generally east, I was too numb to feel much of anything at all. It was a good thing Geraldine sent me away right off. If I had had a night to sleep on it God only knows what I would have done, but I was on the road before I knew exactly what was happening and there was never a point where I could turn back.

I kept wanting to for the longest time. But that was the one thing I knew I couldn't do. I just couldn't go back there again.

The car was a good one, old as it was, and plain driving was a good way to get away from yourself while getting away from Bordentown. I hadn't realized they made Cadillacs with stick shifts, even back in 1954. I don't suppose they made very many of them. The ones they made, they did a good job with. I got the hang of shifting pretty quickly, and after that there was nothing to do but drive.

What I would think about while I was driving, well, the hell with all that. Nothing very brilliant, I don't guess.

I stayed at a motel the first night, and didn't sleep much. It wasn't exactly the Hilton. It was what I think they call a hot-pillow joint, and the room next door to mine was one of the ones they would rent out by the hour. If the walls had been any thinner they would have been transparent. All night long the bedsprings squeaked and groaned, and all night long different men and women told each other they loved each other, and they were all of them lying in their teeth. I don't suppose I would have slept much anyway, but this didn't help.

After that, though, it got easier. One thing the widows' houses didn't have was bedsprings wailing all night long. And I also learned that sleep was a great way to get through time without going crazy. I got so I could fall asleep right away, pulling the sleep over my head like a blanket, and I'd be good for ten hours, sometimes more. I never used to sleep that way before and never have since, just burrowing into sleep and sort of using it.

Every day Bordentown was a few miles further south and east and one day deeper in the past. You just let the past slip away from you and one day you turn around and it's out of sight.

It's that simple, and that hard.

I wrote three letters, one to Sheriff Tyles, one to Geraldine, one to Lucille. This was just a game I was playing with myself because I knew I didn't intend to mail the letters. What was interesting was that the one to Geraldine was the hardest to write. I would have thought it would be the other way around. I tore them all up when I was done, and tore the pieces into smaller pieces, as if the FBI might come around and try to put the stupid letters back together again like jigsaw puzzles.

I also wrote a letter to Hallie telling her about the whole business in Bordentown. I actually expected to mail that letter when I was done with it, and I took a lot of time trying to get it just right, and of course when it was through I tore it up, too.

I did send Geraldine a postcard. I sent her a couple of them at different times. I could never once think of anything to write, so I would leave the message part blank or else just run the address across the whole length of the card. Miss Geraldine Simms, The Lighthouse, Bordentown, South Carolina. And the zip code, which I don't remember, but I knew it at the time.

A lot of the time when I was driving there would be hitchhikers on the road, guys alone or two of them together or sometimes a guy and a girl. Back when I did a lot of hitching I would always promise myself that if I ever had a car I would never pass up a hitchhiker. And the people who gave me rides generally mentioned that they had thumbed their way around when they were younger, and that was why they felt they had to stop for me in return, even though they knew that it was supposed to be a dangerous thing to do.

Now I had a car, a big car with nothing but room in it, and there were all these people on the road, I never went a day without seeing a dozen of them, and I never once stopped. There were soldiers in uniform and hippies and straight-looking kids and older people, everything, and I passed them all up. Not because it was dangerous to stop, although I guess it is, but because I just didn't want to talk to anybody.

It was a funny stretch of time. I guess I wouldn't want to go through it again.

FOURTEEN

I HAD TO WRITE THE LAST CHAPTER
twice. The first time I did it, I put in a six-
page scene that never happened. It was the
first night after I left Bordentown, when I
stayed in the motel with cardboard walls. The
way I wrote it the first time, there was this
long scene where I listened to a couple
through the wall, and the guy finished before
the girl was satisfied, and he just left her
there, and she was storming around the room
throwing things and crying. So then I went
next door and brought her back to my own
room and took her to bed, and afterward she
was sleeping and I heard the same thing happen again in the room next door, except this

time the guy was drunk and passed out before he could do anything. Whereupon the heroic Chip Harrison went next door and found the second girl, and she was also ready to walk up the wall and across the ceiling, and good old Chipperoo brought her back, too, and balled her in the bed while the first girl was still sleeping, and then the first girl woke up, and the three of us had this wild orgy with everybody doing everything to everybody else all at once.

I filled up six pages with that crap. It was a pretty good scene, actually, and I think it would have been pretty erotic.

But I thought about it and tore it all up and did it over the way it really happened.

So I wrote that scene, and it didn't bother me while I was writing it. In fact while I was typing it all out I could actually believe it really happened. Sometimes it's a little frightening the way your imagination will take a lie and make it almost true.

Then why did I tear it up? I could say it was because I didn't want to put any lies in this book, but that's not it because there are already a couple of lies in it that I'm leaving in. Just small lies, but that doesn't make them true. The real reason, I think, is that putting in a scene like that would just make a lie out of everything that happened in Bordentown and lot of what went on afterward. Because that scene I wrote could never have happened. If the beginning of it happened, and if a guy did leave a girl there all unsatisfied, I never would have gone next door. Not the way I felt. If anything I would have just left the motel and gotten back in the car and kept on driving. And if I *tried* to do anything with a girl just then, if somehow I really did make an effort, I'm sure I couldn't have managed to accomplish it.

I didn't leave my heart in San Francisco, but for a while there I guess I left my balls in Bordentown.

FIFTEEN

I GUESS I KNEW ALL ALONG I WAS ON
my way to Wisconsin. In fact the first night
out I tried to figure out just how long it
would take me to drive there if I drove sixteen hours a day and slept eight. (If I had
tried it, I think I would have killed that Cadillac in a matter of days. It was good for another fifteen years if you didn't push it more
than fifty or a hundred miles at a stretch, but
it tended to burn oil when it overheated and
I would have thrown a rod or burned out a
bearing sooner or later.)

But the thing is that I wanted to be going
to Wisconsin but I didn't want to get there. I
wanted to see Hallie. I always wanted to see

Hallie, ever since that one night in September when she came to my room over the barber shop. The next morning she went to Madison to start college, and ever since then I had been not quite going there to see her.

Because if I went there, and if it turned out that there was nothing there for me, then what would I do? I wouldn't have Hallie to send postcards to, or to write letters to and not mail. Or to think about the way knights used to think about the Holy Grail.

Once I was out of Bordentown I really didn't want to see anybody right away, Hallie included. I knew that there had to be some time in between Bordentown and whatever was going to come after it. I don't mean that I spelled all of this out in my mind, but when I think back on it I can see it was something I must have known.

So I took my time, and took down a lot of storm windows and put up a lot of screens, and touched up woodwork and repaired furniture. And before long it was June and the colleges were out for the summer, so there was no point in rushing up there because she would be away on summer vacation.

Of course I knew where she lived, in the

same town where I originally met her, a little town on the Hudson between New York and Albany. It stood to reason that she would go home for the summer, and I suppose I could have gone to see her there, but the way I looked at it was that I was already out in the Midwest and it would make more sense to stay there and see her in Wisconsin when the fall term started.

Which meant that all I had to do was kill a couple of months. I didn't even have to pretend I was on the way to Wisconsin. All I had to do was kill time, and I was getting pretty good at that.

I think some of the pressure came off about the time that the school year ended in Wisconsin. I don't know that one thing had much to do with the other. Maybe it did and maybe it didn't, but within a week after the end of the semester, I did something I hadn't done since I left Bordentown.

By this time I was starting to worry about it. Not that I wasn't doing it—because let's face it, I had gone almost eighteen *years* without doing it, so a couple of months off wasn't anything remarkable. But I didn't even *want* to do it. I didn't even particularly *think* about it, for Pete's sake, and it's usually all I *do* think about.

In fact, I wasn't even doing what I had told Lucille it was perfectly normal to do.

I would see a pretty girl on the street, say, and I would tell myself, *There's a pretty girl.* I still had the brains to realize this. But what I wouldn't tell myself was, *Man, would I ever like to ball that chick until her eyes fall out of her head.* And that sort of thing had always been my normal response to a pretty girl, and now it didn't happen, and I was beginning to worry.

For months I had been with Lucille five days a week. The same girl, lunch hour after lunch hour, and I never once got tired of it. I was always ready and willing and able, and it was always good, and I always enjoyed it. And now it began to seem possible to me that (*a*) I was never going to want it again with anybody or (*b*) I was only going to want it with Lucille. And both of these things amounted to the same thing, because I was never going to be able to see Lucille again.

And if (*b*) was true (and it might have been, I couldn't tell, because I wasn't sure I still

wanted to make love to Lucille but I couldn't
prove that I didn't, either) then it stood to
reason that leaving Bordentown had been a
mistake. But not one of those mistakes you
can do anything about, except maybe cut your
throat, which still seemed a little too extreme.

So it reassured me when it finally happened. And it's reassuring me right now, because I can write about it, and if I didn't have
some sex in this book pretty soon I suppose
Mr. Fultz would give it back to me and tell
me to use it to line a birdcage or something.
He may anyway.

I hope not.

It was in Iowa. I don't remember the name
of the town. (There's another lie for you. I
remember it perfectly well, but I'm not putting it in.) The house I was staying at this
time was like most of the others, a sprawling
old place in the middle of town with bay windows and gables and extra rooms that were
nicely furnished and everything, but nothing
happened in them and nobody ever went in
there. This house had two widows instead of
one. One of them was about sixty, a plump
little old lady with cataracts and hardly any

chin, so that her face just curved back from her mouth to her neck. This took a little getting used to.

The other widow was her daughter. Her name was Mrs. Cooper, and her mother's name was Mrs. Wollsacket. Mrs. Cooper was about thirty-five and she had a perfectly good chin and no cataracts. She also had a son, who was about seven years old and retarded. Very retarded. They had to feed him with a spoon and he would drool most of it out, and his eyes never seemed to focus on anything.

Between the kid and his grandmother's nonchin, I had more or less decided not to look for anything that needed fixing. After breakfast Mrs. Cooper left for work and I got ready to go, and when I went to pay Mrs. Wollsacket she started talking about all the things that needed doing, and how difficult it was to make do without a man around the place, and how here it was June and the second-floor storms were still on the windows. (Incidentally, somebody is missing a good bet; if someone would only sell combination aluminum storm windows to all those lonely old ladies, half their worries would be over.)

Well, I couldn't just leave. It wouldn't fit

the Lone Ranger image at all to run off yelling "Hi-yo, Silver!" without changing those storm windows for her. I offered to do the job for her in exchange for the two-fifty I owed her and another day's room and board. She said, "Oh, I wasn't asking *you* to do it, Mr. Harrison," and I started to say, well, then, I guessed I'd be on my way, and she said, "but I'm surely glad to take you up on your generous offer," and I was locked in.

It didn't take long. I took care of the storm windows and took apart a lamp with a broken switch and put it back together again so that it worked, which completely amazed her. Then I ate a sandwich for lunch and walked around town until I found the library.

The librarian looked vaguely familiar, and when she gave me a tentative smile I realized it was Mrs. Cooper. We had a dumb conversation, and then I looked around until I found a couple of early Nero Wolfe mysteries that I couldn't remember if I had read or not. Mrs. Cooper told me I could take them back to the house even though I didn't have a card. I read them in my room.

One of them, anyway; it turned out I had read the other one.

They fed the kid early, thank God. Then the three of us had dinner and I talked about how I was a student at the University of Wisconsin on summer vacation, and trying to see something of the country and possibly earn a little money toward next year's tuition. (I had been saying this since the term ended. Before that I was the same student at Wisconsin but had dropped out in January for lack of funds and hoped to go back in the fall.) I couldn't tell you very much about the dinner conversation because it was basically the same as all my dinner conversations, and I had learned to handle my end of it without paying much attention to anything but the food.

Afterward I took a loose leg off one of the dining room chairs and glued it back on. This went over well. Then I went up to my room and read the other Nero Wolfe, the one I had already read once before. I had forgotten how it came out and was willing to find out all over again.

Around ten there was a timid knock on the door. I opened it, and it was Mrs. Cooper. She was a little bird of a woman, as thin as her mother was fat, with a slightly pinched look around her eyes and nose. She was prettier than that sentence makes her sound, and would have looked very nice, I think, if she had done something intelligent with her hair. It was the color of a field mouse and she had it pulled back into a bun.

"I couldn't sleep," she said, "and I thought you might like a nice cup of tea, Mr. Harrison."

We had tea in one of the living rooms. Mrs. Cooper talked about how nice it was to work at the library, except that so few people actually read books anymore, with so many of them wasting their time in front of television sets. And she talked about how lonely it was in that town, and how she had wanted to leave, but she couldn't leave her mother all alone and besides there was the boy to consider, and she guessed she would just stay there while life passed her by.

"This must be a lonely summer for you, Mr. Harrison," she said.

"It is," I said. "But I do meet a lot of people."

"I'm sure you must."

"Yes, I do." Brilliant, Chip. If you're supposed to be the Lone Ranger, why do you talk like Tonto?

"I suppose you meet a great many lonely women."

"Uh," Tonto said.

She folded her little hands under her little breasts. "You must bring them a great deal of excitement, Mr. Harrison. Excitement that is sorely missing in their wretched and cloistered lives."

Her eyes were shining weirdly, and she moistened her thin lips with her tongue.

I said, "Well, I guess I change a lot of storm windows, if you can call that excitement."

She leaned forward and put her teacup on the coffee table. She did this very deliberately, as if it would slide off the table unless she placed it in just the right spot. I realized suddenly that she was not wearing the same dress she had had on at dinner. And she was wearing lipstick, and hadn't been wearing any at dinner.

She stood up and crossed the room and sat on the couch beside me. She folded her hands and rested them in her lap.

"My husband died eight years ago," she said.

"I'm very sorry."

"But there is still a fire in me," she said. "My fire has never been quenched."

She put her hand on the front of my pants.

I tried out a lot of lines in my head, like asking her how her husband died, or how long she had been working at the library, or if she thought it would rain tomorrow. Somehow none of them seemed like the right thing to say. I considered telling her that I was a fairy or had been wounded in a campus riot or that I had syphilis. It was like having absolutely no appetite and then having somebody put a plate of boiled turnips in front of you.

"My fire burns for you, Mr. Harrison," she said. She really said that. "Oh, Chip, darling!"

And her hand did things, and of course nothing happened, and I thought, well, maybe I can sort of move the turnips around on my plate. Because while I was sure I would never be able to rise to the occasion, so to speak, I also figured there was more than one way to skin a cat, or quench a fire, and if she had gone eight years without it she could probably get off without too much trouble if I just went through the motions.

So I kissed her.

* * *

The way it started out, I was like a Boy Scout helping her across the street. But somewhere along the way everything changed. It really surprised me. I opened her dress and touched her and kissed her, and in the course of it all I began to groove on her body.

It was a much better body than you would have expected. It didn't look that great—she was much too thin and didn't have much of a waist, so that she was almost a straight line from her shoulders to her feet. Her skin was very soft and smooth, though, and there was no fat on her, and, well, her body just *felt* nice. Some do and some don't, and hers did.

Maybe what I got was a contact arousal from her, because she was certainly excited and she certainly made it obvious. Anyway, I was on the couch with her, just going through the motions, when all of a sudden I realized that I had an erection.

And I thought, Hey, where did *that* come from?

God knows where it came from. But even I knew where it was supposed to go, and it suddenly seemed absolutely essential that I put it there as soon as I possibly could. It didn't seem to matter if she was ready or not, although I guess she must have been ready for the past eight years. All that mattered to me was to get into her, and I shucked my pants and rolled on top of her and jabbed at her with all the subtlety of a tomcat.

It went straight in on the first shot as if she had a magnet in her cervix. She wrapped her arms and legs around me as if she was scared I would take it away. She had nothing to worry about. I kept taking it a little ways away and then putting it back, as fast and as hard and as deep as I could.

Throughout all of this, there was something slightly schizophrenic about the whole thing. Because it was as though there were two Chip Harrisons. One of them was banging away at the poor woman as if he was trying to splinter her pelvic bone, and the other was sitting in a chair on the other side of the room, watching the whole thing and not quite believing what he was seeing.

It went on for a long time, this totally un-subtle relentless sledgehammer screwing, and she came about half a dozen times, and then so did I.

"We'll go to your room now," she said. There was a little puddle on the couch. She put a doily over it, put her dress and my pants over her arm, and took my arm with her free hand. "We'll go to your room," she said, "and do it some more."

"Uh—"

"We'll fuck," she said. "We can try differ-ent positions. I would like to try it with me on top, if that's all right with you. That way you can pinch my breasts while we do it. You may pinch them as hard as you like. I won't mind."

"Uh—"

"You may even bite them if you like."

"Your mother," I said.

"She sleeps very soundly."

"Well, uh, I'm not sure I can do it again. It took a lot out of me."

"I know. Most of it is running down my leg."

"Uh."

"You'll be able to," she said confidently, giving my arm a happy like squeeze. "I just know you will."

She was right.

Afterward, it seemed as if there ought to be something to say. I asked her about her husband, and if he died before the kid was born. Seven months before the kid was born, she told me.

And how long had her mother been a widow?

"Eight years also."

"That's really terrible," I said. "You must have lost them both about the same time."

"Exactly the same time."

"Gee," I said. "An automobile accident, I suppose."

"They committed suicide." She was lying on her back. She had taken her hair down and it looked much better. The pinched-in expression was gone from her face. Sex certainly does wonders for a woman's appearance.

218

"You probably don't want to talk about it."

"Oh, I don't mind," she assured me. "It happened the very day I told them that I was pregnant. That very day, I told them, my husband and my father, and they went downstairs to the basement and into the tool room, and they got the shotgun, and they put the barrel in their mouth and pulled the trigger and blew off the top of their head."

"Oh."

"I was never married," she said.

"Oh."

"It started when I was twelve. He came to my room and told me I was a big girl and it was time I learned how to fuck. I hope you don't mind my using that word."

"Not at all."

"And then he fucked me. I didn't like it, but my mother said it was my duty because he was my father. She read from the Bible. About Lot and his daughters. I didn't like it at all for the first few years, but then I got to enjoy it pretty well."

"Oh."

"What I didn't like was he would always pull it out just before the end. And when he couldn't in time I was always lucky, until one time when I was twenty-six years old and I found out I was pregnant and he shot himself." She thought for a moment. "I don't see why he shot himself," she said reasonably. "There was no need."

"Oh."

"I went to Kansas City, and then mother told everyone that I was married, and I had the baby, and then mother told everyone that Mr. Cooper was killed in an airplane crash and I would be coming back to live with her. But I think everybody knows. Wouldn't you think so?"

"Maybe."

"I think they must. Especially with the baby being an idiot and all. I wish they had told me right away he was an idiot. I would have drowned him. But by the time I knew about it I was attached to him and I couldn't do it. That happens, you know. You get attached to them, even if they are."

She went silent then. Thank God. After a while I said, "Uh, I'm kind of exhausted. I have to get to sleep, and you probably ought to go to your own room. I mean, you wouldn't want your mother to find out about this."

"Why not?"

"Well," I said, "I would be embarrassed."

"Oh," she said. She thought about it, then nodded. "All right," she said, and off she went, her dress over her arm.

I was just falling asleep when the door opened again. There she was, carrying a cup and saucer. No dress this time. She was still naked.

"I brought you a surprise," she said gaily.

"If that's my tea, I don't really want it."

"It's not," she said.

"I still don't want it."

"Well, it's not for you."

"Huh?"

"Lie down and shut up," she said. "It's for the surprise."

"What surprise?"

"You'll see. You'll like it."

"Look, all I really want is to go to sleep."

"You can go to sleep in a minute. Lie down."

"What's in the cup?"

"Just warm water," she said, and filled her mouth with it, and leaned over me.

*   *   *

Oh, the hell with it. I wasn't going to mention it but it's too perfect, and if it ruins her reputation that's just the way it goes. I don't think she'll mind, anyway.

It was Waterloo, Iowa. I swear to God.

SIXTEEN

THERE WERE SOME OTHER GIRLS DURING
the rest of the summer. Some I got to and
some I struck out with.

None of them were very important.

SEVENTEEN

I DROVE INTO MADISON A COUPLE OF weeks after the fall term started. I would have gotten there earlier but I kept putting it off until finally I knew it was time. The old Cadillac got me there in good shape. I started looking around for a tourist home like the ones I had been staying in for the past half a year, and I drove around for a long time without seeing any of the usual signs. Then I remembered that Madison was a university town, and that people with rooms to rent would take in college students by the year.

And I also remembered, just about the same time, that if Hallie was here and stuck in some dormitory it might be pretty stupid to room with some widow. So I got a room at a motel. Sixteen bucks, and payable in advance, and it wasn't even all that much of a room.

I didn't care. I was in pretty good shape financially, with almost two hundred and fifty dollars, which was more than I had had when I left Bordentown. Even with all the gas that the old car burned, I had been earning money faster than I spent it.

I unpacked in my motel room and put my clothes away. I took a shower and shaved, although I had already shaved and showered in the morning. Then I got dressed and noticed I was sweating, and I took another shower and put on a clean shirt and made myself stretch out on the bed and calm down so I would stop sweating.

The campus was huge. It sprawled all over the place. There were a lot of kids sitting in groups under trees and other groups of kids hurrying here and there. I couldn't understand how they could possibly find their way around. It was immense.

I asked a lot of people various dumb questions until someone told me where you could find out where a student was staying, and somebody there told me what dorm she was in, and various other people pointed me toward it.

I went and stood in front of it. I didn't know whether it was all right for me to go in or not. I thought of stopping some girl on the way out and asking her to find Hallie for me, but instead I just waited.

And then two girls came out, and one of them was Hallie.

She looked exactly the way she had looked a year ago. Exactly. She was wearing dungarees and a sweatshirt and sandals, and her granny glasses made her brown eyes look even bigger than they were. Her hair, straight and glossy brown, was a year longer than it had been.

I said, "Hallie?"

She looked at me, and stared, and said, "Chip?"

I nodded, waiting for her to run up and throw herself into my arms. (I had rehearsed this scene a lot.) She didn't exactly do this. What she did was say something to the other girl about seeing her in class, and then she walked slowly toward me, a smile spreading on her lips, and reached out her hands for mine.

Her hands felt small and very soft.

"I can't believe it," she said. "When did you get here?"

"About an hour ago."

"Are you going to be studying here?"

"No."

"Oh."

"I was in the area," I said, "and I thought I would drop in and see you."

"Wow, that's really great. Oh, wow. Like I can't really believe all this."

"Yeah."

"I got your cards. I was going to write to you, but there was never a return address."

"Well, I never stayed in one place very long."

"Oh."

"I wrote you a couple of letters, too."

"I never got them."

"I never mailed them."

"Oh."

"You look fantastic."

"So do you. You filled out a lot, didn't you? You were thinner. You didn't used to be so big in the shoulders, did you?"

"I guess not. Hallie—"

"Could we sort of walk this way, Chip? I have this class."

"Oh, sure."

"I suppose I could cut it."

"You don't have to do that."

"Well, I really shouldn't. They keep a record of cuts. It's pretty idiotic but they do."

"I don't want you to get in trouble."

"It wouldn't be trouble, exactly—"

"I mean, it's not as if I have to be on the road in an hour or anything. I mean, I could meet you after class."

"That would be great."

"What is it, an hour?"

"Uh-huh. If you could meet me out in front? By the step over there?"

"In an hour. Sure."

"Great."

You want to know something? I wasn't going to write all this shit. I had it planned differently. The last chapter, Chapter Sixteen, only has twenty-seven words in it. (In case you forgot: *There were some other girls during the rest of the summer. Some I got to and some I struck out with.* Paragraph. *None of them were very important.*)

Well, it wouldn't have been a hell of a lot of trouble to take those twenty-seven words and make twenty-seven pages out of them. Or even more. Because whether what happened for the rest of the summer was important or not, it might have been mildly interesting. One time I double-dated with this farmhand. We took out two sisters and each screwed one of them and then traded girls and screwed them again. I had never done anything like that before, and it would have been interesting enough to make a scene out of. It would have made a damned good scene, as a matter of fact.

So there would have been plenty to write about, and the book would have been long enough to stop with me just getting to Wisconsin, or just getting ready to drive to Wisconsin. That was the way I originally planned to do it.

Hell.

That would have been cheating. Because the way this book ends, the way I'm ending it now, is sort of the point of it. Or part of the point of it.

But it's a fucking pain in the ass to write it. (They may take that line out. I hope not.)

*   *   *

I went someplace and had a hamburger and a cup of coffee. On one side of me some students were talking about the draft lottery, and on the other side some students were talking about Gay Liberation. They already seemed liberated enough to me.

I was back in front of the building two minutes before the hour was up. Those ten minutes took another hour. Then some clown rang a bell and a few seconds later people started coming out of the building. Eventually one of them was Hallie, and she came over to me and held out her hands again, and I took them again. I asked her how the class was, and she told me, and we wasted a few words on that kind of garbage.

Then I said, "Is there some place we can talk?"

"My room?"

"I don't know. Am I allowed there?"

"I'll allow you."

"I mean—"

"We have twenty-four hour open halls," she said.

"I thought maybe we could go for a ride."

"Oh, you've got a car?"

"Uh-huh."

"Okay."

When we got to it she said, "Wow, a Cadillac! Look who turned out to be rich."

"It's a '54. I mean it's worth maybe fifty dollars."

"It looks great. When did you buy it?"

"I got it in the spring. Somebody gave it to me."

"Oh."

"It runs pretty good, though."

"I didn't know they made them with standard shift."

"I think this may have been the only one."

"Maybe it's an antique or something."

"I suppose if I keep it long enough."

"Yeah."

There was a lot more brilliant conversation like that. I just drove around forever without paying much attention to where we were, and we kept trying to get conversations going, and they kept being like what I quoted. She told me what courses she was taking and I told her some of the places I had been, and I kept getting more uptight about the whole thing, and I guess she did, too.

At one point I said, "Listen, I have this

room. You know, a motel room. I mean we could talk there."

"Oh."

Eventually there was a red light and I stopped for it. I turned to her and said, "I don't mean to ball or I would have said it, but I want to open up and rap with you because we have to, and I don't want to do it sitting under a tree or in your dormitory or in this fucking car."

"Okay."

"You don't mind?"

"No, of course not. It's weird, isn't it? A whole year, and we never really knew each other."

"It'll be all right."

It was still a little awkward at first, partly because the bed took up about eighty percent of the room, and there was only one chair. No matter how much you say that you just want to talk, in a situation like that it's hard to pretend there isn't a bed in the room. I had her sit on the chair and I sat on the edge of the bed.

It wasn't really rapping at first, but it got there. I told her some of the things I had done. I especially told her about Geraldine and the Sheriff, and how I had sort of become the child the two of them had never had together.

She told me about her brother, who had been in the service when we met, just on his way overseas at the time. They sent him to Vietnam and he was on a patrol and stepped on a landmine.

"It happened in the middle of December. But they waited until I came home for Christmas vacation before they told me about it. We were just starting to get close that summer. Before then, you know, an older brother and a younger sister, we never had that much to say to each other. And now I'll never get to talk to him again. Sometimes I think I'm beginning to get used to it, and then I find out that I'm not."

And later she said, "I never knew you were a writer. *No Score.*"

"Huh?"

"No Score."

"You lost me."

"Your book," she said. *"No score,* by Chip Harrison. I read it about a week ago."

"It's published?"

"You didn't know? It's all over the stands. All over Madison, anyway."

"That's really weird. I even forgot about it. I mean, I kept looking for it and it never turned up, and I guess I thought they decided not to bother. They didn't pay me very much money and I thought they decided to write it off. What was the title?"

"*No Score.* Don't you even remember the title?"

"I had a different title for it. I guess they decided to change it. It's been about a year since I wrote it." Then something occurred to me. "Oh," I said. "I guess you read it, huh?"

She nodded.

"It wasn't very good, huh?"

"I thought it was good." She had a funny look on her face. "I never expected to be in it, though."

"Oh."

"You didn't even change my name. I thought you could get in trouble that way, not changing names."

"I changed everybody else's name."

"What made me so lucky?"

"I just couldn't think of another name for you," I said. "It was just *Hallie Hallie Hallie* in my mind and I couldn't think of you any other way."

"You put down the things we did and everything. The words we said to each other."

"I didn't think anybody would know who it was."

"Oh, of course not. How could they? Hallie from the Hudson Valley who goes to school in Wisconsin. How could anybody possibly figure out it was me?"

"Oh, wow."

"It's okay, Chip."

"Yeah, it's sensational. I never even thought. I didn't think about anybody reading it that I would actually know. Or that was in it."

"It doesn't matter."

"It doesn't?"

"No. Honest." I looked at her, and she was smiling shyly. "I never guessed it was your first time. With me, I mean."

"Oh. Well, it didn't seem like something I wanted to announce."

"When I first read it I was furious."

"I can imagine."

"What really got me was that I couldn't even write to you and tell you how mad I was. I wrote a letter to your publisher just the other day. If they send it to you, you've got to promise not to read it."

"They wouldn't know where to send it."

"I guess they'll send it back to me then. I'll tear it up." Her face opened. "But after I stopped being mad, I guess it made me proud. Do you know what I mean?"

"I hardly remember what I wrote, Hallie."

"Maybe I can refresh your memory," she said. She stood up and took off her sweatshirt.

I said, "Last time you were wearing a bra."

"I got into Women's Lib a little last spring. I decided they were generally full of shit, but they're right about bras. Do you think I need one?"

"No."

She kicked off her sandals, unfastened her dungarees. "You've still got all your clothes on," she pointed out.

"Hallie, we don't have to. Honestly."

"Don't you want to?"

"Yeah, but I don't think you do."

"Would I do it if I didn't want to?"

I looked into those big eyes. "You might,"

I said. "You might just because you thought you should."

"I really want to, Chip."

"Come here."

I kissed her and felt her breasts against my chest. For some reason or other I felt like crying. I kissed her again and let her go, and she took her dungarees off and I started to get out of my clothes.

We made love.

She had her eyes closed. I put my hand on her stomach. She was shiny with sweat.

After a while I said, "Tell me about it."

"Huh?"

"What went wrong?"

"Huh?" Her eyes opened. "Nothing went wrong. I had an orgasm."

"I know."

"So?"

"So you weren't really there. You were somewhere else and it wasn't right."

"Oh, wow."

"Or else I'm a little flaky, which is possible."

"No."

237

"I'm right, then."

"Yeah. Shit."

"What's the matter?"

She turned away. "I didn't think you would be able to tell. I guess that was pretty stupid, thinking that. I'm sorry, Chip."

"There's nothing to be sorry about."

"Yes there is. The thing is, oh, I don't know—"

I waited.

"The only way is to say it. I have an old man."

For a minute I thought she meant her father. I had spent the past nine months with people who were several years behind on their slang. Then I realized what she meant and I said, "Oh. A guy."

"Uh-huh."

"Well, I figured you would be seeing guys. And the rest of it, as far as that goes."

(This was a lie. Not that I had ever expected that Hallie would be sitting up in Wisconsin saving herself for me. But I just managed never to think about her with anybody else. I don't much like to think about it now, if you want to know.)

"I'm sort of involved with him."

"In a heavy way?"

"Kind of heavy, yeah."

"Oh."

"Like we're living together."

"Oh." Why did I suddenly feel as though I was dying? "For very long?"

"Well, we were sort of together starting in April, but not actually living together. And he was in New York for the summer, he lives out on the Island, and we saw each other a few times during the summer, and when we came back to campus we started, uh, living together."

"In your room?"

"No. He has this apartment off campus. I keep some of my clothes and things at my room because there isn't much space at his place. But I sleep there, and cook meals and like that."

"Oh."

"I don't think it's a forever thing or anything, but, oh, I dig him, you know, and it's very much what I'm into right now."

"Sure."

She turned to me. There were tears running out of her eyes but she wasn't really crying, and the tears never got anywhere near her voice.

She said, "I'm really a bitch. I should have told you out in front and we never should have balled. Maybe all I really am is a cunt."

"Don't talk like that."

"I just don't want you to hate me and you've got every right in the world."

"Why should I hate you? I *love* you, why the hell should I hate you?"

"Oh, *shit*," she said, and this time she let go and cried.

EPILOGUE

October 17, 1970

Miss Geraldine Simms
c/o The Lighthouse
Bordentown, South Carolina

Dear Geraldine:

Awhile ago I sent you a copy of a book I wrote called *No Score*. I hope you got it, because otherwise this won't make too much sense. Or maybe it will—it seems to me I told you most of what happened in *No Score* at one time or another.

Anyway, along with this letter I'm sending you the carbon copy of another book I wrote.

I just finished it. In fact I haven't finished it yet, I'm finishing it right now.

If you read *No Score*, you may remember that there was an Epilogue at the end that told what happened to me after the actual story of the book ended. I decided the other day that this book ought to have an Epilogue also and I couldn't decide exactly how to do it. While I was trying to work it out in my head I also decided I wanted to write you a letter, and I thought about it some more and decided that, in a sense, this whole book was a letter to you. So I'm killing two stones with one bird.

What I hope you'll do now, Geraldine, is read the carbon of the book all the way through and then come back to the letter.

Did you go back and read the carbon copy? Thanks. And if you didn't, I forgive you. I never heard of a letter with an intermission before.

After Hallie said *Oh, shit* and started crying, that was about it. Of course in books it can just end like that (which is why I ended it like that) and in life it can't, because the two people are stuck there in the room and, unless the boiler blows up and kills them all, they still have certain dumb unimportant things they have to say to each other, like while they're putting on their clothes.

Just as an example:

"You know, Chip, you would really like him. I mean it, you ought to meet him sometime."

"No way."

"No way you could like him or no way you could meet him?"

"Right both times."

"Yeah."

That kind of dialogue, Geraldine. It was tons of fun, believe me. I had a wonderful time.

Then I drove her back to her dormitory, and then she insisted that I wait while she got the copy of my book so I could autograph it for her. I wanted to drive away but I also wanted to see her again.

I won't tell you what I wrote in the book. I wrote something, and closed the book, and told her not to read it until later. She nodded.

"Well," I said.

"Chip."

"What?"

"Write to me."

"Should I?"

"And this time put a return address."

"Really? All right, sure."

"Chip? It was the timing, I think. I mean, oh, you know what I mean."

"Sure."

"I mean, people like us, we'll probably run into each other again."

"We probably will."

There was more but that's enough. I went back to the motel and packed because all I wanted to do was drive away from there, though I was afraid to trust myself on the road. But I couldn't sleep either.

I thought about getting drunk but if you were between eighteen and twenty-one all they would serve you was beer. I was a couple of days short of nineteen but my ID said I was a couple of days short of eighteen. Maybe they would have served me beer anyway. I didn't really care because I didn't think I could get drunk enough on beer, not the way I felt.

Do you remember the glass of corn whiskey you gave me that last night? That's what I really wanted.

I sat around there for a while feeling numb and empty and lost and alone. I had never felt this alone before because there had always been Hallie somewhere in the distance, and now there wasn't. It didn't feel good.

Then I remembered my book. *No Score.* I had hardly looked at the copy I signed for Hallie. I left the motel and went to drugstores and bookstores looking for it. It was really weird seeing it on the stands. My name all over the place, on the spine and the cover and at the top of every even-numbered page. I wanted to buy all the copies they had, but who was I going to give them to? I bought one copy and took it back to my room and read it.

What a strange feeling. Here was this kid talking, and he was me, except he wasn't, because when I talk to myself it's something that happens inside of my head, and this kid was talking on a page. Well, quite a few pages, actually.

And he sounded so young. It was just impossible to believe that this punk was me. And just a year ago.

Poor Hallie. It must have been really traumatic to read all that, especially when she had no idea it was coming. I guess on all those postcards I never mentioned anything about writing a book, or that somebody was going to publish it.

I guess the book settled me the way liquor might have. I read it all the way through and then I got undressed again and went right to sleep.

I left Madison early the next morning. I drove east and almost stopped in Chicago but changed my mind at the last moment and took the Belt around the city. I burned a lot of oil but kept stopping for more so that I didn't do any damage to the car. It still runs perfectly, by the way.

I drove all the way to Cleveland. I guess I was ready for a big city again. I put the car in a parking garage and took a hotel room and paid a week in advance. I was in no hurry to go anywhere.

It was easy to find things to do. I would go to a movie and when it ended I would go to another one. I bought paperbacks and read them. Sometimes they seemed to be sending me special messages. I would find great personal meaning in very ordinary things. But I recognized this as just a temporary mild madness and let it pass.

That's the thing. You don't outgrow that kind of garbage, but you learn to see it coming. Maybe growing up is largely a matter of being surprised by fewer things.

Everywhere I went I would see copies of my book. I wanted to tell people I wrote it, but who was I going to tell? I sent you a copy (which I really hope you got) and I sent a copy to the Headmaster of Upper Valley, the asshole who threw me out. I told what a fink he was in the book and I wanted him to read about it.

I couldn't think of anyone else.

Then one day I was looking at ads for jobs, and I could find some things that I probably could do, but I didn't want to do any of them. And I said, Wait a minute, I'm a published author.

I think that's the first time it occurred to me to write another book. I spent a day or two trying to work out a novel but every idea I came up with was corny, and then I thought maybe I could do the same thing I did in *No Score* and just continue that story. I didn't know if the material would be as good, though. It seemed to me when I read it that *No Score* was pretty funny, and my memories of the past year weren't.

I guess that brings it all up to date. I bought a typewriter in a pawn shop and got some paper and started writing. At least this time I knew about keeping a carbon.

The book got written faster than I thought it would.

Well, that's about it. Now I'll drive to New York and let Mr. Fultz look at this. I could sell the car and fly there, I suppose, but I don't like the idea of selling the car. Because you gave it to me.

Geraldine, I read through all of this and it feels very funny. All those changes. There are things I wonder about and can't know, like what happened with Lucille, whether she was really pregnant, whether she had an abortion or had the baby, whether she put it up for adoption or decided to keep it. I have this persistent fantasy in which she keeps the baby as a memento of her dead lover. That would probably be the worst thing for everybody, but evidently my ego gets a boost out of it.

One thing that's bad is that I still can't get away from the idea that sooner or later Hallie and I are going to wind up together. I suppose I'm fooling myself but I can't get it out of my head.

I don't know what comes next, but you never do, do you? Just one damned thing after another. Thanks for suffering through this. It's a pretty funny letter, but then the whole thing adds up to a pretty funny book.

I was just looking at *No Score* to see how I ended it, and it went like this:

I hate it when the author steps in at the end of the book and tells you what it was all about. Either you find it out for yourself or it's not worth knowing about. So I'll just say goodbye and thanks for reading this, and I'm sorry it wasn't better than it was.

That makes a good ending for the book. And for the letter, too.

Love,

Chip